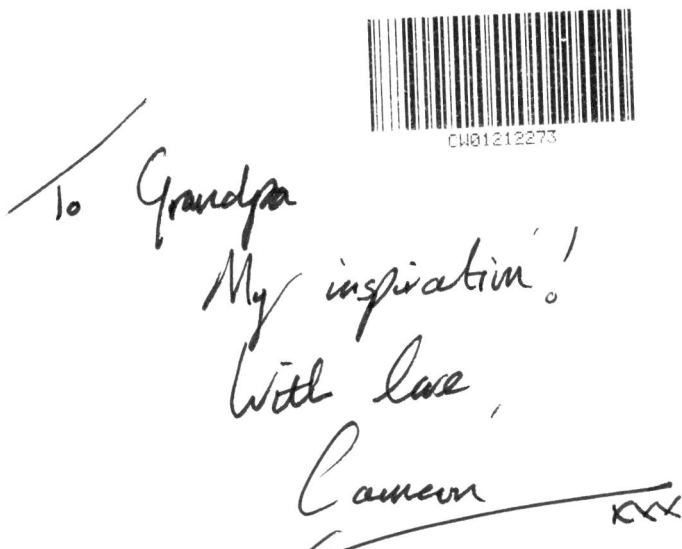

To Grandpa
My inspiration!
With love,
Cameron
xxx

RED LIES

CRISTELLE COMBY

ALSO BY CRISTELLE COMBY

The Neve & Egan Cases

RUSSIAN DOLLS

RUBY HEART

DANSE MACABRE

BLIND CHESS

Vale Investigation

HOSTILE TAKEOVER

EVIL EMBERS

AVENGING SPIRIT

GHOST SHIP

TIME AGAIN

Stand Alone Stories

RED LIES

ALONE TOGETHER

ALSO BY CRISTELLE COMBY

Short Stories
PERSONAL FAVOUR (*Neve & Egan* prequel)
REDEMPTION ROAD (*Vale Investigation* prequel)

The short stories are exclusively available on the author's website: www.cristelle-comby.com/freebooks

Copyright © 2020 by Cristelle Comby
This book is a work of fiction. Names, characters, places and incidents, other than those clearly in the public domain, are fictitious. Any resemblance to actual events or real persons, living or dead, is purely coincidental.
All rights reserved.

No part of this publication can be reproduced or transmitted in any form or by any means, electronic or mechanical, without permission in writing from the author.

Edition: 1

ISBN: 979-8643210993

Credits
Cover artist: Miklstar

DEDICATION

To my cousin, Virginie, who decided one day to move to Sweden and on whose shoulders befell the responsibility to introduce me to this charmingly beautiful country and its kind and welcoming people.

Tack så mycket!

"The worst lies are the lies we tell ourselves."
RICHARD BACH

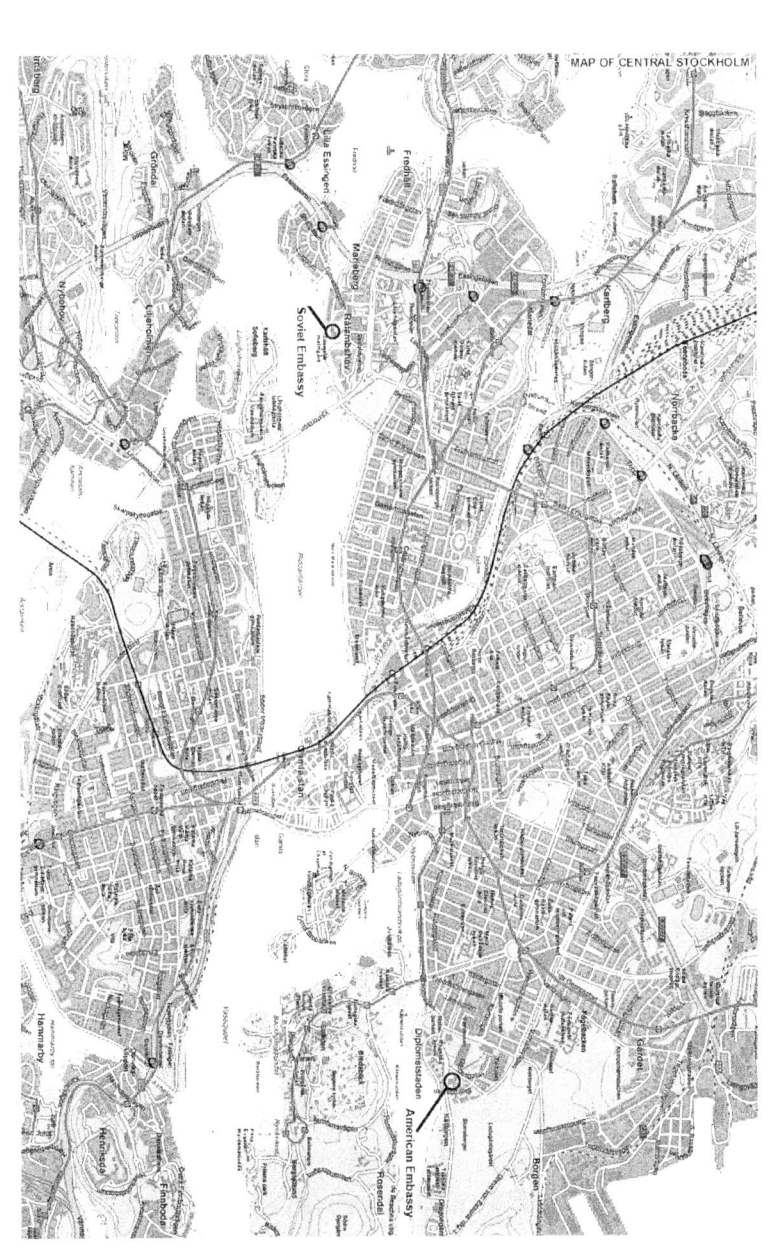

CONTENTS

Wednesday, February 19, 1986	1
Friday, February 21, 1986.	11
Wednesday, April 2, 1986.	17
Friday, April 4, 1986.	21
Saturday, April 5, 1986.	35
Sunday, April 6, 1986.	39
Friday, April 11, 1986.	49
Sunday, April 13, 1986.	59
Tuesday, April 15, 1986.	67
Wednesday, April 16, 1986.	73
Saturday, April 26, 1986.	81
Monday, April 28, 1986.	91
Sunday, May 4, 1986.	95
Monday, May 5, 1986.	99
Friday, May 9, 1986.	107
Friday, June 6, 1986.	115
Sunday, June 8, 1986.	121
Monday, June 9, 1986.	129
Friday, June 13, 1986.	135
Sunday, June 22, 1986.	141
Thursday, June 26, 1986.	147
Friday, June 27, 1986.	155
Sunday, June 29, 1986.	159
Tuesday, August 1, 1986.	163
Friday, August 9, 1986.	169
Sunday, August 11, 1986.	183
Monday, August 12, 1986.	191
Thursday, September 3, 1986.	207

Note From The Author	213
Further Reading	214
Further Reading	216
Further Reading	218
About The Author	220
Keep In Touch	221

WEDNESDAY, FEBRUARY 19, 1986

MOSCOW, USSR.

Sofiya Viktorovna Litvinova awoke with a start, her eyes popping open. It took her a few moments to realise someone was pounding on the door. Pushing her tangled dark hair out of her face, she grimaced at the bad taste in her mouth. Glancing at the alarm clock on the bedside table, she had to blink several times to make out the time: it was four in the morning.

Struggling to get out of bed without tripping on the bedsheets, she left the warmth behind and groaned when her bare feet touched the cold concrete floor. Sitting up, she noticed from her bedroom window that snow was falling outside. Though it was almost the end of February, spring was still a long way away in the Soviet capital.

The furious drumming continued; she wrapped herself in a blanket to hide her nudity before crossing through the bedroom. Entering the small kitchen, which doubled as a living room with a couch and a bookshelf, she flicked the single ceiling lamp on. The drumming only stopped when she opened the front door.

In the doorway was a short-legged forty-something man with sharp features and calculating dark eyes. He was dressed in a crisp uniform, impeccable despite the early hour.

Mikhaïl Alexandrovitch Serov set foot in the doorway without asking permission.

"Pack your bags, my little bird. We're going to Sweden." Entering the flat further like he owned the place, the black-haired man moved to the kitchen to pour himself a glass of water.

Sofiya, who still had the door handle in her hand, blinked back her surprise. Serov was her superior at the *Komitet Gossoudarstvennoï Bezopasnosti*—the KGB, and when she was in the field, he acted as her liaison officer. But this week, he was supposed to be on leave—and so was she. Closing the front door, the young woman turned back to him, a puzzled expression marring her delicate face.

Serov seemed to notice her outfit—or lack thereof—for the first time. Without bothering to hide it, he gave her slim figure an appreciative glance before continuing, "We have a new mission."

"No one to charm this time, I hope?" she asked, though she feared she already knew the answer.

Serov's twisted thin-lipped smile was all the answer she needed. "They are sending you, little bird, aren't they?"

The FCD—the First Chief Directorate—had singled her out when she was only a teenager. With her long legs, blossoming curves, and wide green eyes, they'd known right away that they could put her looks to good use. She hadn't disappointed, growing up to become a very alluring woman. She had lean, toned limbs and curves in all the right places, a long slender neck, and an oval face with delicate features.

Her deep green eyes shone above high cheekbones and a charmingly innocent smile that could brighten even the gloomiest of days.

As the youngest daughter of two farmers living in the outskirts of Moscow, joining the service was the best future that the fifteen-year-old girl could have hoped for. Her mother had been thrilled at the prospect of having one mouth less to feed. Better still, her sweet daughter would be serving the nation with warm clothes on her back and a full belly—courtesy of the Motherland. No, Yelena Litvinova could not have dreamt of a better future for her baby girl.

Little did the old woman know that after a rigorous—at times torturous—training, Sofia would join the flock of ravens and swallows at Directorate K: the secret Counter-Intelligence Department of the FCD. Behind the innocent bird monikers hid the most deceitful spies the Soviet Union had on offer. Polyglots, cultured, and natural-born liars, the agents of Directorate K were trained to blend in and adapt to the most demanding of surroundings, be it a palace's dining hall or a prison cell. Versatile, charming, and masters of disguise, they used everything and everyone to reach their goals, be that an innocent mark or their own bodies.

Her mother had gotten it partially right: her daughter's belly was full most of the time. But she rarely had clothes on her back when she performed her duties for the Motherland.

Sofiya leaned back against the front door. "I'm supposed to be on leave," she said, crossing her arms over her chest.

"As am I," Serov replied. "But our presence has been requested."

What's new? she thought bitterly. At thirty-four years old, she'd spent nearly a third of her life infiltrating foreign networks to gain information and ensure the safety of Soviet embassies all over the world. By now, she knew days off were a rare commodity.

"What's the mission?" she asked, moving to the bedroom.

"Things are tense between Moscow and Stockholm right now. The FCD has been asked to take a closer look at our embassy employees and their allegiance."

Sofiya frowned as she reached for the suitcase she kept under her bed, ready to leave at all times. "I thought Sweden was neutral."

"It is," Serov confirmed, "But they're a little ticked about some of our submarines darting a little too close to their coast or something."

Serov's voice was too loud for him to be speaking from the kitchen, and Sofiya turned to look over her shoulder; she found him leaning against the bedroom doorframe.

"Our embassy is only twenty minutes away from the Americans. And our little investigation has revealed some irregularities." He sighed. "Moscow wants us to take a closer look at one of the diplomats."

Sofiya moved to the wardrobe. "Why don't they just eliminate him?" She pulled out a pair of fresh underwear and her grey-brown uniform. "Or is it no longer the standard response?"

Serov gave no intention of moving or averting his gaze. "He's from the *Nomenklatura*."

Sofiya was no prude, and she'd done worse with her body than strip in front of a man, but she was loath to give Serov a free show. The blanket only came off after she'd pulled on her panties and bra. The shorter man's lustful gaze followed her every move.

"I thought the time of the Tsars was over," she said, stepping into her pencil skirt, which fell just below her knees.

"Except that he has connections and money—a lot of it. He was born into it." Serov smiled an appreciative smile when she bent down to tie her boots. "The Motherland wishes that this fortune stays within its confine rather than fall into the wrong hands."

"Perish the thought," she muttered as she reached for her cap.

They were in Serov's car less than five minutes later, northbound to the FCD offices where they would be presented with a full briefing.

Sofiya should have relished this opportunity to cross the Iron Curtain, but she was in a foul mood at having seen yet another day off cancelled. She knew she was expected to feel pride at doing her duty for her nation and her comrades, but, deep down, she felt used. Nowadays, it seemed that no matter how pretty she looked or how nicely she dressed, she always felt dirty. Truth was, she hadn't felt really clean in years, despite lathering up with a good many bars of soap when she got back from a mission.

On her way out of the briefing, she yielded to her only pleasure in this dreary life and headed to her favourite bar. She pushed the door open and saw that the place was almost empty. Aside from the bartender behind the counter, there were only two men seated at a table by the window.

Sofiya headed for the bar where wooden stools butted up against the brass foot rail of the high counter. She climbed on one, crossed her bare legs, and put her cap on the tin counter.

The bartender, a balding man with a thick belly, faced her

with a warm smile. "Comrade Litvinova. The usual?" he asked, knowing better than to question her reason for being here.

It was only ten in the morning, but she already wanted to wash the day away; it had begun with Serov entering her apartment, and his lascivious gaze when he'd watched her get dressed. A cold shiver ran down her spine at the memory. She hated the man. She'd hated him since the first time he'd tried getting between her legs—and she'd said no—eight years earlier.

Serov was a pervert, but she knew how to handle men like him. She knew how to handle all types of men; the FCD had taught her that. It was all about understanding their deepest needs and desires—and then giving them exactly that.

Her superior liked his whores to be young and shy; she had found out one night as she trailed him through dark streets. Though she was already twenty-six when he was assigned to her, he'd have enjoyed taking her to bed—if she'd agreed to play the frightened little bird for him, which she hadn't. It was with a show of confidence and without breaking his gaze that she'd turned him off. Her attitude and words had been neither childlike nor shy, and he'd soon gotten the message.

For the time being, Serov was her superior, but she'd long since learned that things changed quickly in their line of work. And who knows, maybe one day she'd get the order to slit his throat.

Sofiya looked at the bottles and upside-down glasses in the racks above the bartender's head, and the very visible laminated governmental notice that informed her that alcohol consumption was forbidden in the mornings. "The usual," she confirmed.

The bartender's smile widened, and he fetched a label-less bottle from under the counter. "One very strong glass of water, neat—coming right up."

When Mikhaïl Gorbachev was elected General Secretary of the Communist Party the year before, one of his first actions had been to curtail the consumption of alcohol in the entire Soviet Union. The prices of beer, wine, and vodka went up, and shops were only allowed to sell alcohol between 2 pm and 7 pm.

Funnily enough, that did little to stop the drinking. If you knew where to go, you could still purchase alcohol at all hours, including at "drunk corners" and from cab drivers—not to mention the frequent appearance of bootlegged surrogate alcohol and home-made booze. But Sofiya was a traditionalist, and she liked drinking her vodka pure—no matter the hour.

The midday sun was high in the sky when both FCD officers arrived at the military airfield. Their ride, a twin-engine cargo aircraft, was ready and waiting for them on the tarmac.

With her suitcase in one hand and her uniform cap in the other, Sofiya looked at the plane with some trepidation. The faded off-white paint and numerous scratches and bumps made it look like something Aeroflot put in production in the early forties. Serov hadn't seemed to mind, and he'd climbed the steps without pause. Trusting that her government knew what it was doing and had its agents' safety at heart, the young woman followed him inside.

She found her superior seated in the left-hand row, pouring himself a drink from a miniature bottle. He'd packed several bottles, she noted, but gave no sign of wanting to share one with her. Serov was aware of her penchant for stiff drinks, and she supposed he wanted her sober to discuss the mission; a good thing she'd stopped at the bar on the way, then.

The pilot entered the cabin and locked the airplane door behind himself. Without a glance in their direction, he moved to the flight deck. Looking around, Sofiya noted that they were the only passengers in the twenty-seater. The intercom buzzed to life an instant later, and a gruff voice announced, "Prepare for take-off, please."

She fastened her seatbelt and let her gaze wander outside. The right propeller whirred to life in front of her eyes, and she felt the plane start to move. In the distance, the countryside zipped by at increasing speed and was soon replaced by a sea of grey clouds.

"Did you read the file?" Serov asked once he'd finished his drink.

"Of course," Sofiya replied, annoyed he'd asked. She may not like this mission or having to work with him, but she was still a professional. And she would give this assignment her best, as she always did.

"Glad to hear," the man said, opening a second miniature. "Let's hope you will not forget where you are this time."

Staring at the cloudy skies, she clenched her teeth to avoid saying something she might regret later. Once, she'd made a mistake. Once. But it looked like Serov would use every opportunity he could to remind her of that lapse in judgment.

It had happened two years ago when she'd been wrapping up a job in eastern Switzerland. She was ready to board a train to head back home when an overzealous guard asked her for her credentials. Her cover was that of a college student from Winterthur visiting Zurich, and she had the documentation to match. Only when she'd given it to him, she spoke in German, momentarily forgetting that the locals only spoke Swiss German. Though both languages had similarities, they could hardly be mistaken for each other, something she'd learned the third year of her formation. Had she been sober, she would never have made such a blunder. But she'd allowed herself two shots of a local brew to celebrate the end of a successful assignment. It took her a lot of sweet-talking and a quickie in the men's room with the guard to get out of that train station without handcuffs. Now, it was a black mark on her ledger, and that ordeal served her as a reminder to stay off the booze while on a mission.

"Also, nowadays, people who are caught drunk at work or in public will be prosecuted," Serov reminded her as if he guessed at her thoughts. "And we wouldn't want that, now; would we?"

Things change, she remembered, as she clenched the fingers in her lap into fists, *and men like Serov sometimes die in tragic accidents.*

FRIDAY, FEBRUARY 21, 1986.

STOCKHOLM, SWEDEN.

In the back of a flower-delivery van, Sofiya was dressed to the nines. She had swept her brown hair up in a bun and adorned her slender neck with a thick pearl necklace. A long emerald-green dress with a deep cleavage hung close to her shapely hips.

She checked her makeup one last time in her pocket mirror before turning the ceiling lamp off.

"It's about time," muttered Serov from behind the wheel.

"Beauty cannot be rushed," she explained, as she placed the compact back in her purse.

The driver looked at her reflection in the rear-view mirror. "Got everything?"

"Of course." She turned her back to him and moved to the back door. "See you at the rendezvous point."

With that, she left the van and crossed the street to a nearby building. In the cover of darkness, she pushed open a small wrought-iron gate and crossed through a courtyard unseen. Even in the dim light, she could see that the Östermalm domain facing her was imposing. There was no one around, and she sneaked to the backdoor that had been used all day for deliveries. At precisely ten o'clock, she knocked three times on the large wooden door. A dark-skinned man in a waiter's uniform opened and ushered her in. Without a word, he led her through the larder and into a small corridor that opened into the reception hall.

Serov had spent the last two days organising everything. For all his sleaziness, Sofiya had to admit that when on a mission, he was efficient. While she'd brushed up on her Swedish at the hotel, he'd procured them with a means of transportation and greased enough hands to ensure she'd make it to her target without question.

The house she was in—which many would call a small palace—belonged to a local nobleman, Lars de Cointreau. He was the descendant of a French *Marquis*, and he liked to flaunt his title at every opportunity. To that effect, he frequently hosted eccentric parties to which most of the Stockholmian upper crust was invited. Tonight, the guest list included the Russian ambassador, his chief of staff, and their target.

The reception hall was impressive: a vaulted ceiling embellished with scalloped edging, plaster medallions, and custom mouldings loomed over a glossy hardwood floor. Four large marble columns lined the room on both sides.

Sofiya acted like she'd just returned from a trip to the restroom and moved like she belonged here as much as any other guest. Entering the hall, she discovered that next to each column stood a caged animal. The closest one held a jet-black panther that seemed to want to be here as much as the Soviet secret agent did.

With her head held high and her shoulders tucked back, she mingled with the other guests. The results of years of posture training were in full display when she reached for a glass of champagne from a passing waiter. She brought it to her lips with grace and a delicate arching of her hand—a gesture not unlike that of a seasoned ballerina. Beauty could easily catch the attention of men, but she knew it took something more to ensnare them. And she'd spent years perfecting that something more.

Moving to another marble column, she discovered, at its feet, a white tiger. The caged animal was nervous, roaming left and right as much as it could within the confined space. It was obvious the poor beast wanted out, and it would have gladly sunk its teeth into the first fat bourgeois it found.

A man got a little too close to the cage, and the tiger roared in his direction. The two women by his side giggled in delight. Disgusted, Sofiya thought the two tarts in fluffy dresses looked like ostriches and could have benefited from having their own cages.

Moving forward, she kept looking for the face of the man she was after: he had short-cropped blond hair, high cheekbones, an aquiline nose, and hard-set lips. She had memorised the photograph she'd been given down to the last freckle, but the diplomat was nowhere to be found. It didn't help that a lot of the local Scandinavian guests shared many of the Slavic traits she was looking for.

It was the eyes that she recognised first—calculating, icy blue pupils that felt like a cold street on a winter morning. Viktor Petrov, Counsellor at the Soviet embassy to the Kingdom of Sweden, stepped into her field of vision, and she took an instant to assess her target. The uprightness with which the tall, athletic man walked was impossible to miss, and evidence of his aristocratic ancestry shone in his every move. Dressed in a dark blue suit with fine white lines, the thirty-nine-year-old diplomat stood out from the crowd with his height and allure.

Sofiya aimed for the red panda caged to the man's right. Timing her steps so that their paths were sure to cross, she missed a step midway and tripped on purpose.

As intended, Petrov caught her with ease, and she clung to his rescuing arms more than was necessary. Through the rich fabric of his suit, she felt strong muscles undulate beneath her fingers as he helped her find her balance.

"*Förlåt mig*," she said, in flawless Swedish. "Two drinks, and I cannot walk straight anymore." Still half in his embrace, she looked up to thank him and found a face unlike what she expected. There was no smile on the man's lips, no warmth to his features. It was as if he'd caught her more out of reflex than out of any real interest.

Well, thought Sofiya, *this will be more difficult than I thought.*

Untangling herself, she blinked her coal-circled, moist green eyes at him. "Malin Waldenström," she said, reaching out a delicate hand to him. "And whom might you be?"

His voice was deep and cold, as he replied, "Viktor Petrov—but you already knew that."

She blinked her incomprehension at him, lowering her hand when it became obvious that he had no intention of shaking it.

"You can drop the act; I know what you are," he continued in Russian, *sotto voce*. "With your tight-fitting dress and swan-like face that would drive any lesser man crazy, what are you, Directorate K?"

Sofiya swallowed thickly and fought not to let her mask slip. Who the hell was this man, she wondered, and how could he have seen through her so quickly? Or had he been warned that someone from Moscow was coming?

"I'm loyal to the Motherland and the cause," Counsellor Petrov continued. "If there's a leak at the embassy, it's not coming from me. Now go home, *little swallow*."

The demeaning nickname and the acerbic tone with which it was said grated on her nerves, but she fought not to let that show. Giving up on any plans to seduce her mark, she quickly switched tactics and reverted to her native language, too.

"Fine, you know why I'm here. Then also know this: I will not go home empty-handed." Inching closer to him, she whispered in his ear, "Give me something, or I'll stick to you like a second shadow."

When next she crossed his gaze, she seemed to catch a hint of challenge in Petrov's light-blue eyes.

"You know what it'll be like," she continued. "Wiretaps, photographs — I'll have my eyes on you like a satellite in the sky, just like that new MIR station they launched yesterday."

"I am, and have always been, loyal to my country." Petrov looked down his nose at her, contempt dripping from his every pore. "If they want proof, tell your superiors that I have devised a way to activate plan TJ–9; that ought to do it."

The code-word meant nothing to her, but Sofiya committed it to memory.

"I believe this concludes our little discussion," he said, before reverting to Swedish. "*God kväll, fru* Waldenström."

Before she had time to reply, Petrov had already stepped away to join a group of men massed in front of the white tiger. Sofiya had no choice but to let him go. Before leaving, she reached for another glass of champagne, which she downed in one go. TJ–9 better mean something to her superiors, or she'd be walking home empty-handed.

WEDNESDAY, APRIL 2, 1986.

MOSCOW, USSR.

Leaving the bourgeoning warmth of spring behind, Sofiya pushed open the wrought-iron gates of the unwelcoming FCD building. It was a massive concrete building punctured by rows of small barred windows and made up entirely of sharp angles and straight lines.

Dressed in a crisp uniform, she saluted the young officer minding the security checkpoint without stopping. In the foyer, she drew in a breath before taking the stone steps to the higher floors two at a time. It wasn't often than an officer like her was summoned to the top floor, and she wondered what fresh hell awaited her there.

She reached her destination at the end of a long, carpeted corridor, lined with pictures of the highest-ranking members of the *Komitet*—past and present. She took a minute to rearrange her uniform before knocking on the door. The order to enter was immediate, and she stepped inside.

The rectangular office was large and sparsely decorated. A window on the left-hand side illuminated the room, and a corkboard took up nearly all the space on the opposite wall. Maps, pictures, and a variety of documents were pinned to it in an assortment of clean rows and columns. On the wall opposite the door stood three filing cabinets and a large oak desk.

Sofiya noticed two men waiting for her there; one of them was sitting with a clutter of documents in his hands, and the other was standing a little to his right. From where he stood, Mikhaïl Serov gave her a curt nod of acknowledgment. The man seated behind the desk, the head of Directorate K, didn't lift his head.

Sofiya stood straighter as she waited to see what fate would befall her. The Comrade Director had only ever talked to her once—the day she joined the ranks of Directorate K—and now, there she was, summoned to his office. Taking in a deep breath, the young officer saluted, introduced herself, and came to stand two feet from the wooden desk.

"You're going on a long-term mission," the balding man told her without looking up.

Sofiya swallowed, hard. A dozen questions burned her tongue: *What kind of mission? Where? And for how long?* She silenced her thoughts and kept her mouth shut.

"Your target," the director said. With a wrinkled hand, he pushed forward on his desk the photograph of a man. From where she stood, Sofiya couldn't make out the person's traits.

"It seems that despite his apparent cooperation, he continues to hide things from us. Some of his associates are questionable, and there are money deposits we couldn't trace." Nose still in the documents, the director paused to flip a page. "We do not know if he's acting alone, or if he has allies within the embassy. Directorate K is counting on you to find out."

Without moving from where she stood, Sofiya leaned forward to better see the photograph; she was surprised to recognise Viktor Petrov.

"You've been trained for this," the director continued. "Make him fall in love with you; play the part until his suspicion evaporates. Insinuate yourself in his life and send us detailed summaries of his activities. Record every conversation you can." The list went on.

Though she knew the only thing they expected from her was her obedience, Sofiya asked, "How long will my infiltration last?"

That got the director's attention, and he looked up from his file for the first time. His bushy grey eyebrows narrowed as he fixed her with a stare that could have made the sun shiver. "Indefinite duration."

Sofiya closed her eyes for a short moment, the breath caught in her throat. Indefinite—it could last ten years or more.

"The Swedish Prime Minister is staying in Moscow for a couple of days, and Petrov accompanied him. Comrade Serov has arranged for you two to meet again. The Soviet Union thanks you for your service."

The director looked down at his file again, and Sofiya knew a dismissal when she saw one. She saluted and headed out of the door without another word. The walk from the corridor to the stairs seemed longer this time, and all the way down, she had to hold on to the staircase railing to not lose her balance. Echoes of the director's words rang loudly in her ears.

Indefinite duration.

Nursing a drink at her favourite bar, she forced herself to remember such things happened. A long-term assignment had always been a possibility; hell, in her line of work, it was a matter of 'when', not 'if'. And she'd reached the right age for that, too.

She was getting too old to bait dignitaries into compromising one-night stands. But she was the right age to settle down and start a family while she played the long game.

She'd heard the stories of agents who had created a whole new life for themselves in the West, getting married and bearing children to their targets to better cement their new identities. She'd also heard the stories of the Communist Party later converting these children to the cause.

She emptied her glass and signalled the bartender for a refill.

FRIDAY, APRIL 4, 1986.

MOSCOW, USSR.

Paperwork was one aspect of her job Sofiya never cared much about. The thorough post-mission reports she'd been required to write every time she returned home always felt like a punishment—the last unenjoyable part of an overall questionable occupation. But paperwork was another cog in the machine, a task she was required to perform—and so she did. Her reports were meticulously drafted and forgotten the instant she left them in her superior's in tray.

She'd never given much thought to what befell those loose A4 sheets of paper after she'd parted with them. For her, they ceased to exist the instant they left her hands. Little did she know that that was not the end of their journey; they continued to exist for quite some time, never actually disappearing.

As she stood in front of the entrance to the non-descript building that served as the *Komitet*'s centralized archives, with a bundle of documents tucked under one arm, Sofiya wished she'd remained in the dark about the paperwork's final destination.

Pushing the large oak door open, she entered with her head held high and a neutral expression on her face. She was dressed in her uniform and removed her cap when she reached the security desk.

The young man seated there asked for her credentials with a warm if droopy smile. Sofiya had the feeling his position required him to be more alert than he was, but then again, given where he was stationed, she could see why boredom could be tempted to settle in.

He let her in, no questions asked, and Sofiya took the elevator up to level three. There were five floors to choose from that were above ground, and another three that were below ground, housing the more sensitive data. Eight floors of archives; eight floors of shelves and boxes and dust. Eight floors of dead silence and immutability where nothing ever happened. She'd just found her personal hell.

The elevator dinged and opened its doors, and the smell of old paper and dust made her cough in surprise. Predictably, there was no one in sight, and she let her displeasure show on her face as she entered the archive.

She found a cart and unloaded the files on top of it. Then she started walking through the sections, looking for the final resting place of the reports she'd been given.

This wasn't the FCD section—these were stored below ground—but contained rather more innocent matter, such as international relationships, trading, and economics. These were not subjects that could have ever interested a counter-intelligence spy like Sofiya. But she could see how these could appeal to a man such as—Viktor Petrov, for instance.

That she knew his superior had asked him to carry out some research on the possibility of broadening the gas trade in Scandinavia, and that a particular report had been drafted on the subject two years ago, by an analyst, was fortuitous. That she knew he'd been asked to fetch this report before flying back to Sweden tomorrow, and that he hadn't yet—so it was obvious he would drop by sometime today—was just Sofiya being good at her job.

Sofiya was down to her last file and contemplated taking all the documents she'd archived out of their boxes again to restart the whole process when suddenly, the sound of the elevator doors opening and closing interrupted her.

It was soon followed by the tip-tapping of footsteps on the cold hard floor. The gait was hard and rhythmic, masculine. The sound grew closer to her, and she readied herself for the task she had really come here to perform.

Feigning indifference, she reached for a random box on the tallest shelf. Standing on her tiptoes, she leaned forward and held the position until she caught movement in her peripheral vision. Sofiya resumed her motion, taking down the box before crouching to place it on the floor.

"Well, well, well—wouldn't that be my little swallow?" Viktor Petrov asked, in a tone she couldn't decipher. He'd stopped at the beginning of the section in which Sofiya crouched.

Opening the box's flap with one finger, Sofiya turned to face him with a controlled mix of surprise and annoyance.

"Comrade Petrov," she noted, pushing a folder inside the box. "I'm going to end up thinking you're following me."

Leaning against a row of cardboard boxes, the diplomat chuckled. "If I remember correctly when we last met, it was you who was looking for me."

Standing back up, box in hand, Sofiya let him think he'd won the point. "May I know what a gentleman such as yourself comes to do in the archives?" she asked, her tone forcefully cold. "Don't you have any dust-free hands to shake?"

"I have some documents to consult," he said. "And what is your reason for being here? I didn't know field agents archived."

"They don't," confirmed Sofiya, feigning annoyance. "Except, of course, when they get reprimanded for coming back from a mission empty-handed." She punctuated her words with a dark look in the man's direction before stretching to place the box back on the top shelf. Guilt-tripping the mark was a classic ploy, and it worked every time.

Petrov hesitated for a moment before stepping closer to her. "Oh, is it because of the Stockholm mission?"

The young spy wasn't lying when she said, "Yes, it's all your fault."

"You see my confusion," he admitted, thinking it true. "How can I make it up to you?"

"You could help me with the archiving," she suggested, turning back to face him, hands on her hips, an eyebrow raised in a mock challenge.

He burst out laughing, which pissed her off. *These nobleborn, they're all the same,* she thought disdainfully—*too good for grunt work.*

"I can't do this," he said, serious again, "but I can try to make up for it later. How about I invite you for dinner?"

"I'm not interested in you." Sofiya started to turn her back on him. Playing hard to get was also high in her book of tricks.

"I said *invite you*, that is to have a drink or eat something, not sleep with you."

With a seductive pout that was intended to be perceived as fake, she turned back to face him. "Oh, so you're not interested in that last part, are you?"

"No," Petrov shook his head. "You're out of my league; I know that much."

Turning on his heel, he called out over his shoulder, "But the invite still stands. Call me for the details; I'm sure you'll have no trouble finding my number."

"Damn *Nomenklatura*," she muttered between clenched teeth as she retrieved her empty cart and pushed it towards the exit. "Always feeling so entitled."

Predictably, Viktor Petrov had taken the bait, but Sofiya refused to smile at her victory. She would have preferred that her little mind-game was discovered and that this whole charade was put to a premature end.

In a vacant office of one of the Kremlin eastern towers, Mikhaïl Serov finished cleaning his Makarov pistol with a small piece of cloth. He and Sofiya had been cooped up in the austere room for two hours, and he'd chosen to use this opportunity to clean his service weapon.

"He's leaving tomorrow," Serov said, loading a fresh magazine. "Tonight's your only chance to persuade him to take you with him, little bird." He pressed the lever on the left side of the frame, and the slide released, loading a cartridge into the chamber. "I suggest you play the damsel in distress and let him be the one who saves you from this cruel life."

"Thanks for your help," she said with an eye roll. "But I know what I'm supposed to do."

Eight o'clock was fast approaching, and Sofiya paced the room in circles like a caged animal. Her mind flashed back to the panther and tiger at the Marquis' home, and she wondered at what had happened to the wild creatures. They had probably been moved to other iron cages they so desperately wanted to escape from. She knew how they felt and shared their yearning for a taste of freedom.

Inspecting his handiwork with an approving nod, Serov said, "Our first meet-up will be in two months unless you have something urgent to communicate." He engaged the manual safety mechanism before placing the Makarov back in its shoulder holster. "We need him to lower his guard first before you can activate."

"I know how it works," Sofiya confirmed. "Make him fall in love, marry him, and then stab him in the back."

Serov raised an eyebrow at that.

"Figuratively," she amended.

"For now," the senior officer said, standing up.

The wall clock ticked eight, and he opened the door for his colleague. Feigning sincerity, he said, "I'm going to miss you, little bird."

She turned on her heel and walked out without sparing him a glance. "I'm afraid I can't return the compliment," she tossed over her shoulder.

Sofiya had never been in the Grand Kremlin Palace before, and she marvelled at the opulence she discovered inside. It was so unusual for her country.

Georgievsky Hall, one of the palace's five reception halls, was longer than most churches she knew. Named to commemorate the Order of St. George, the long rectangular hall was lined with snow-white columns and intricately carved niches. A dozen massive golden chandeliers hung from the high arched ceiling, their light reflecting in the glazed, ornate wooden parquet.

The massive hall felt oppressive to her, and she would have felt lost in the sea of dignitaries massed around the various buffets had she not been at Petrov's arm. The tall, blond man was dressed in a clean-cut navy suit. For once, Sofiya had been allowed to wear something more feminine than her service uniform. The clothes had been selected for her by Serov, and looking at the other women present, she saw that they suited the event.

It wouldn't do to be too provocative at such a prestigious event, and a large mink cape covered her bare shoulders; even her hands were gloved in black velvet. Beneath the cape, she wore a long auburn dress, a little larger fit than she was used to, but one that still offered ample cleavage.

"Well, Comrade Litvinova, how do you like your evening?" Petrov asked as he directed them to a buffet filled with toasts and caviar. He took two pieces of bread, placed a large spoonful of black eggs on each, and handed one to his guest.

"It's all right," she said before taking a bite. "I've seen better."

"All the elite of the Soviet Union in one room," Petrov chuckled. "And my date is jaded."

Sofiya finished her toast and said, "I'm hard to please."

Petrov saluted an elderly man in a uniform who had just arrived at the caviar stand, and they moved forward, aiming for a buffet covered in assorted seafood.

"Ever tried oysters?" Petrov asked as he grabbed one for

himself. Licking the shell bare, he swallowed it, and Sofiya raised a curious eyebrow at him.

Rising to the challenge, she looked at the variety of toppings and sauces on display and grabbed a shell. She covered the oyster with some onions and a strawberry and swallowed it. The flavours blended together on her tongue in an exquisite mix. Smiling at the man's disbelief, she said, "A French chef taught me all the best ways to enjoy their taste."

"Aren't you full of surprises?" Petrov nodded. "I have to say, you have rather piqued my curiosity," he continued. "And now, I wonder: how does one become a spy?"

"The traditional way," she replied, as they kept moving forward in the grand hall. "They noticed me when I was in school; my parents, who are farmers, agreed to let me go. The next thing I knew, I was enrolled in the FCD program." It was the truth, mostly. She'd only left out the part where she had to abandon everything she knew, her family, and her friends—all to come to live in a secret military compound where she was tortured and pushed beyond her limits—but the Motherland called that training, so what was there to complain about. And she'd gotten out eventually, and into a proper apartment, once she graduated.

"What about you?" she asked, not giving him a chance to question her further. "Why does a high-ranking member of the *Nomenklatura* become a career diplomat? Bored of playing with your silver spoons, were you?"

He grinned at the mention of his debatable ancestry. At the time of the Tsars, people like Petrov held society in the palm of their hands, but now that the masses had turned to communism, they had lost most of their power and influence.

"My mother made sure I received a long and inclusive

education, but one does grow bored of tutelage after a while. When the opportunity to try something else presented itself..." He let his sentence hang. "Turns out that my ancestry *is* an advantage today, as the Swedish Royals prefer to deal with someone of the same rank as themselves."

Sofiya smiled at him, though his words chafed on her nerves. She hated people who thought of themselves as superior purely because they were born into the right family. They were all about enjoying the fruit of the labour of the workforce, without ever lifting a finger to help with the harvest.

They kept moving from buffet to buffet and from acquaintance to acquaintance. Petrov never bothered to introduce his date to the men and women he ran into, and the silences between encounters and bites of food were filled with meaningless chatter.

When the evening ended, the young woman was no closer to ensnaring the diplomat than when it had started. Though he seemed to enjoy her company, Petrov hadn't given her a single opening. Keeping a reasonable distance at all times, filling his hands with either a glass or a plate, he'd made sure she couldn't get promiscuous. Moreover, he'd made sure their discussion topics remained vague and punctuated by long silences.

As he led her to his car, she couldn't tell if he'd enjoyed himself or not. On the one hand, he'd looked at ease during the gathering, smiling throughout and politely greeting the guests he knew. But a part of her couldn't help but think that the diplomat's smiles were as empty as her own.

Petrov's black car turned left at the Kremlin Palace exit and followed the Moskva River south. At eleven-thirty, the streets were deserted, and the man drove away at high speed.

Though she had never given him her home address, Sofiya noted that he'd taken the right direction to drive her home.

When the crude concrete block of flats where she lived loomed in the distance, Petrov surprised her by taking a left turn in a small, unlit, back-alley. She sat straighter in the leather seat but chose to remain silent as she waited to see what he was playing at.

The diplomat parked the car at the end of the road before exiting the ride without a word. He'd left the engine running and the headlamps on, a silent invitation for her to join him in the cold night.

A scent of musky fabric and motor oil hit her when she stepped outside, and she looked around to orient herself. She easily recognised the area; her escort had parked in front of the entrance of a textile factory.

At this late hour, the place was deserted, and Sofiya knew that if she were to scream her lungs out in this place, no one would hear her. That being said, it also meant no one would witness it if Petrov took her hard on the hood of his car. Thinking that she may have misread the signals and that the diplomat was interested in her after all, she slowly sashayed over to him.

In the harsh light of the headlamps, the man looked pale as he turned to face her. "Don't bother," he said in a cold-as-ice tone that froze Sofiya's blood. His smile was gone, as were the kind, amiable manners he'd used with her all evening. "Did the old fool really think I would fall for that? Our chance encounter at the archive this morning, and then you acting like the perfect potential girlfriend all evening?"

Once more, Sofiya was faced with the cold, calculating man she'd met in Sweden. She hadn't fooled him, but he had fooled her. *Why?* she wondered. Why had he wasted his time toying with her like that?

"They still don't trust me," he continued, "even after what I promised them?"

"They doubt your allegiance and question some of your acquaintances," Sofiya confirmed, seeing no reason to lie to him at this point. "Perhaps if you delivered on that promise?"

"I need more time," Petrov said darkly. "And the right person to do the job."

Having no idea what they were talking about, the young woman could offer no insight. She surmised this had to do with the mysterious TJ-9 operation he'd mentioned in Sweden, but no one had bothered to clue her in about the details. But whatever it was, it hadn't been enough to quell the head of Directorate K's doubts.

Sofiya held the man's gaze as she considered which approach to take. He had her at a total disadvantage. Unarmed, in a remote location, she had no choice but to win the game if she wanted to make it out of that alley alive. If only she could understand how this man worked. Earlier, she'd thought she had him figured out, but she'd been wrong on all accounts. Even now, with his controlled, expressionless face, Viktor Petrov remained a mystery. His features were schooled into a perfect picture of placidity; he was a frozen pond in a dead forest on a continent where no one lived.

"I don't know what you're looking for," he said. "But you won't find the answer on my face."

"You had spy training, didn't you?" she asked, coming to the only possible conclusion.

Petrov straightened up and looked down at her. A manufactured smile appeared on his lips, but it held no warmth. It was merely the result of flexed muscles, and it made her think of an automaton who'd just been fed a coin.

"And it took you this long to figure it out?" he questioned. "I would have thought the KGB trained you better than that."

Sophia felt stupid. Why had she assumed that with him being part of the *Nomenklatura*, he would have stayed away from the army?

"A lot of diplomats receive basic training. The fact that I come from wealth hasn't allowed me to escape that," he said, as if reading her thoughts. "Actually, I quite enjoyed my time there and asked for the full package."

"Time well spent, I imagine," Sophia said, not surprised he'd enjoyed learning how to mask his emotions and deceive people.

"Indeed. Unfortunately, I cannot carry out field missions," he continued. "With my past, were I to be caught, the consequences would be terrible—politically."

Or rather you don't like to get your hands dirty, thought Sofiya. "That's too bad; with those sharp cheekbones, you'd have made a fine raven," she remarked, hitting a nerve.

Petrov's voice darkened, the only sign that her words had affected him. "I doubt it. I'm not good at pretending, and I care little for these deceitful games."

"Then why become a diplomat? With the money you have, you could move anywhere and live a quiet life."

Another empty smile bloomed on his lips. "If I told you that it was out of patriotism and devotion to my country, would you believe me?"

Sofiya gave him a mock smile of her own. "No, I wouldn't."

"It is, however, the case," he said.

Silence fell on them again. Aside from the car's engine

purring at their side, there was no other disturbance in the small back-alley—not even a stray animal scavenging for food.

"You're not the only one under scrutiny, you know," she said eventually. "They have me on a tight leash too. Stockholm was a disaster, and the director's making me pay for it," she admitted, looking away from him. "By the looks of it, this, too, will be another black mark on my file."

A humourless chuckle escaped Petrov's lips. "Some honesty, at last."

"You want honesty?" she asked, turning back to face him with a raised accusing finger. "How many black marks do you think the *Komitet* will tolerate?" Sensing an opening, Sofiya continued with renewed passion, "If I go back to them empty-handed, Viktor, I'll be marching to my own death."

"Sofiya, I—"

"You might as well kill me yourself," she cut in. "I know you have a pistol with you, so go ahead and use it."

"Don't be dramatic," Petrov said, taking a step closer to her.

She turned her back on him, hiding her face and the tears that she could feel pooling in her eyes. "There's no other way for it. You either give me something, or you can kill me." She took a step away, then another, and her silky auburn dress undulated in the car lights. "Here and now, Viktor. Make your choice."

The open road faced her, and she wondered if she could walk away. In less than ten minutes, she'd be home. *But what good would that do you?* she asked herself. She was on assignment from the director himself, and he would know if she failed. Mikhaïl Serov may tolerate another black mark, but she knew the director wouldn't.

Behind her, she heard the familiar sound of a pistol being cocked. Viktor Petrov had made his choice then, and Sofiya turned to face him with all the dignity and determination that years of training had ingrained in her. The only thing betraying her emotions was the brightness in her green eyes as she faced the weapon in Petrov's hand.

"I can't give you what you want," he said.

Little emotion showed on the tall man's face, and Sofiya knew he had as little choice as she did. Both of them were pawns—disposable pieces used and abused in a game they had no control over.

"It's all right; I understand," she nodded. "For what it's worth, I don't blame you."

She took a step closer and another, coming to stop inches away from the muzzle of the pistol. From this distance, she knew the shot would be fatal.

Petrov nodded, and Sofiya looked up. The sky was bright tonight, and she wondered when she had last taken the time to look at the stars.

Not a bad sight to die to, she thought, and a shot rang out in the night.

SATURDAY, APRIL 5, 1986.

MOSCOW, USSR.

Sofiya knew something wasn't right when she felt no pain.

She looked down at the pistol in Petrov's hand and saw plumes of smoke leaping out of the barrel. It was aimed at the empty parking lot on her right, she noted. He'd averted his shot, but "Why?" she breathed out, with what little air she had left in her lungs.

"Come with me," he entreated her, raising his hand to aim at her again. "Work for me."

Was he offering her a third option, she wondered, *go rogue, leave the KGB?*

The Communist Party would never forgive her for that; they would hunt her down, and then go after her entire family, just to make an example.

"They won't let me go, Viktor. They made me who I am; I belong to them."

"Don't tell them; let them think they've won." The pistol in Petrov's hand didn't waver. "You've given this country more than it deserves. Come back to Sweden with me—

work for me. In exchange, I promise to find a way to get you out."

Then, using her own words against her, he said, "Make. Your. Choice."

The alarm clock beeped at eight, and Sofiya groaned in her pillow. She had a dry mouth and a killer headache, and it took a while for the room to come into focus after she'd opened her eyes.

Before going to bed, she'd downed half of the bottle of vodka she kept in her fridge, and it hadn't agreed with the champagne, oysters and other delicacies of the evening. After a long moment in the bathroom, she'd finally managed to fall asleep, but her dreams had been plagued by tormented memories and nightmares of the future that awaited her.

With a groan, she stood and stretched her taut back before slipping out of bed. The auburn dress was pooled by the foot of the bed, and she left it there with her high-heel shoes and faux-leather purse. Crossing through the room naked, she entered the kitchen and aimed straight for the fridge. A cold shot of vodka with ginger and lime was the best hangover cure she knew.

She froze when she noticed a familiar figure sitting on her sofa: Mikhaïl Serov.

"Wild night?" he asked, taking in her messy mop of hair and smudged mascara.

She cursed at the sight of him. "Don't you know how to knock anymore, Misha?"

Forcing an innocent look, he leaned forward and said, "Had to make sure you were alone before I showed my face."

"Fuck you," she muttered into the fridge. Uncapping a bottle, she took a long swallow which burned all the way down.

"Have to say, I was a bit disappointed not to find the Counsellor here, sprawled between your porcelain white legs," Serov continued, "or were you too wasted to perform?"

Sofiya closed the fridge hard, then she turned on her heel and left the room. She didn't need to look up to know that Serov's gaze followed her retreating back's every move. *Bet seeing me this way gives him a hard-on*, she thought bitterly before pushing the bathroom door open.

Serov was still on the sofa when she came out of the shower some twenty minutes later. He still hadn't moved when she entered the kitchen dressed in black pants and a thick woollen grey jumper.

She placed a suitcase at her feet. "I'm expected at the airport at eleven. Petrov is taking me back to Sweden with him."

"Wonderful, my little bird," Serov said, with mock pride. "I never once doubted you."

Sofiya chose to ignore his comment. "What's the contact protocol?"

"If you need help, send a letter to your dearly departed aunt," he said, getting to his feet. "I'll know what it means. Then wait two days, and I'll give you a signal to arrange a meeting."

She nodded. "Fine."

"But that's only if something urgent comes up," he cautioned her. "Otherwise, I want you to stay dormant for the first two months. Once that period has elapsed, we can arrange regular information drops and figure out a way for me to give you your instructions."

Two months without having to see this pervert's face! Now that sounded like a real holiday. "Anything else?" she asked.

"Not that I can think of, no." Serov opened the door to see himself out. "Thank you for serving the cause, little bird. And don't mess this up."

She didn't need to be told that twice. Closing the door, she felt trapped between a rock and a hard place. On the one hand was the devil she knew: Serov, the *Komitet* and a world of red lies and deceit. On the other, shrouded in darkness, was the riddle that was Viktor Petrov and his untold secrets. And somewhere between the two, almost invisible to the naked eye, stood the very fine line she'd have to walk if she wanted to get out of this mess alive.

SUNDAY, APRIL 6, 1986.

STOCKHOLM, SWEDEN.

The Soviet embassy was situated at Gjörwellsgatan number 31, in the district of Marieberg, on the island of Kungsholmen. Looking at its dreary austere exterior, you'd never guess that it had once been a porcelain factory.

Petrov had driven past it on the way to his apartment. And he'd explained to Sofiya that the ambassador and most of the embassy staff lived within walking distance of the chancery, in houses and flats paid for by the Motherland.

Petrov himself had been granted the use of a two-bedroom flat located on the fourth and last floor of an apartment building situated on a bay that overlooked Lake Mälaren, the third-largest freshwater lake in Sweden that flows through the capital.

On the living room balcony, Sofiya stood facing the horizon with a map of the city in one hand and a coffee in the other. Committing landmarks to memory, she took in the scenery left to right. A corner of the Västerbron Bridge in the distance, and then the island of Långholmen. A glimpse at the southern suburban part of Stockholm right in front of her, and to her right the island of Lilla Essingen. The landscape here was so different from home, and she knew it would take her time to get used to this meandering city that stretched across fourteen islands. The smallest ones only had two or three roads crisscrossing their surface, while the larger ones housed up to a dozen districts. Moving around town also came with a lot of complications, seeing as there were only so many bridges. With no direct routes, people often had to hop on and off two or three islands to reach their destination.

A cold gust of wind coming in from the south blew her hair in her face, and she shivered. Cradling the coffee mug in her hands, she returned to the warm confines of Petrov's living room.

Though there was nothing ostentatious about the place, it was elegantly decorated. A light-brown couch and two assorted armchairs sat around a hand-carved wooden coffee table. A tall buffet and several wooden shelves completed the ensemble.

On the right, a small corridor led to the front door, and on the left, a longer one led to the twin bedroom suites.

She'd been relieved to discover there were two separate bedrooms and that she wouldn't be required to share a bed with Petrov. Since their discussion in the alley, the diplomat had shone his true colours. Gone was the kind smile and warm face he'd offered her at the Kremlin. Now she was faced with a cold, controlled man who preferred the sound of silence over idle conversation.

That last part suited her fine, and she was relieved to learn that he would be spending most of his time out of the apartment during weekdays. Even better, his position saw him forced to attend several social events in the evenings, and sometimes, during the weekends.

"Of course, it will be expected that I take my girlfriend to the most important ones," he'd said without looking up from the newspaper he was sifting through.

"I will need clothes," she'd replied from where she sat on the sofa.

"I'll give you money for that." He turned a page. "Oh, and go to the hairdresser, too; do something about those bangs—your hair looks too Russian."

Reaching a hand up to brush at the short hair that stopped just above her eyebrows, she'd wondered what a hairdresser could do about it—aside from letting it grow.

"Use your free time to brush up on your Swedish," he'd continued, as he neared the end of the newspaper. "You need to be perfectly eloquent, but keep a slight Russian accent for now. After all, you haven't been here for long."

Their conversation had naturally come to an end when the phone rang. Petrov got up to answer from the privacy of his bedroom, rather than use the unit in the living room. Sofiya hadn't dared try to listen in on it. He left her alone in the flat soon afterwards.

Closing the balcony door shut behind her, she took her empty mug of coffee to the kitchen sink and left it there. She hadn't been here for a day, but already, she felt restless.

After she unpacked, she spent the better part of the afternoon inspecting the flat, on the lookout for hidden cameras or miniature microphones. She found none and had been left with nothing more to do. Itching for some action, she shrugged on her boots and reached for her coat. Petrov wanted her to be familiar with the city and the local language? Well, she only knew one efficient way to do that.

She jogged down the steps, two at a time, buttoning her thick woollen coat as she went. She crossed the lobby, pushed the large glass door open, and froze when she recognised a familiar silhouette in the parking lot.

She ducked behind a low hedge of cypress trees before Petrov had the time to see her. The blonde diplomat stood by the boot of his car, with his hands deep in the pockets of his black coat. He wasn't alone; a woman stood facing him.

Sofiya didn't have time to see her face. Cautiously, she inched closer to the last tree and peered through the needles. She could make out her slim, medium-height silhouette and long, flowing red hair, but she was looking out on the parking lot, and Sofiya couldn't see her face. The anger that radiated from the woman was easy to spot, though. It showed in the tensed arms that she'd crossed over her chest and the nervous booted foot that kept tapping the sidewalk. Petrov had a more relaxed stance, and Sofiya strained her ears to try and make out his words.

"...ready for Friday, don't worry..." the words came and went, carried on the wind, "...natural talent at this..."

The redhead turned her head to face him again, allowing the young spy to discern her features. They were those of a mature woman who'd probably already reached fifty. She had a round face, almond-shaped, coal-rimmed eyes, thick, glossy lips, and a clear penchant to overdo things in the makeup department.

A deep frown creased her brow. "Talent enough to stab you in the back," she said, anger in her tone. She wasn't as soft-spoken as Petrov, and Sofiya had no trouble hearing her side of the conversation. "She is Directorate K, Viktor. You know what that means—everything she sees and hears she will report back to Moscow."

"...long as the assignments are in line with the cause...to worry." Petrov took a step forward and reached for the woman with both hands. He forced her to uncross her arms and took both of her hands in his. "You...too much," he muttered before leaning in close to kiss her fully on the lips. When they parted, he inched closer and murmured something in her ear. The words were lost on Sofiya, but the reactions they had on the woman weren't. The corners of her mouth relaxed, and her eyelids drooped. Whatever he'd just offered was appealing to her. And the way she reached forward, letting go of one of his hands to brush hers against his crotch made the nature of the offer abundantly clear.

Stepping away briskly, the redhead turned on her heel and headed for a light grey Volvo parked a little ahead. She got in, turned the engine on, and drove away. Petrov was right behind her, following her in his own car.

Once they'd both disappeared down the road, Sofiya moved out of her hideout, hands in her pockets as she pondered this new turn of events. Viktor Petrov was having an affair with Svetlana Anatolieva Alexeïeva, the Minister-Counsellor of the Soviet Embassy.

Well, well, well, she thought, unable to keep from smiling, *what in the world am I going to do with that information?*

Petrov was still absent when Sofiya returned from her hour-long walk. She surmised that he wouldn't be there for another hour, at least, and she took a long bath to warm up.

She found him in the living room afterwards when she went to the kitchen to prepare an evening snack.

He joined her and sat at the kitchen table. She stayed at the counter to finish making herself a sandwich before placing the ingredients back in the fridge. She didn't offer to make him one and took a bite of hers before moving to the seat at the opposite end of the table.

"There's a reason Moscow pays such close attention to what goes on in Stockholm," Petrov said, placing both palms on the table as he faced the young woman. "This country has chosen not to take any sides in the conflict that opposes east and west."

There had been no 'how are you?' or 'how was your day?' Rather, Petrov chose to go straight to business, and Sofiya took it in her stride.

"I know that; they're neutral," she said, between two bites. "No need for a geography lesson."

"You don't understand the importance of this," Petrov continued. "We can move about this city as freely as the Americans. We go to the same bars and restaurants. We run into each other at parties, while our wives shop at the same boutiques and frequent the same hair salons."

Sofiya kept chewing as she waited for the punchline.

"The American embassy is in Östermalm, less than twenty minutes away. The ambassador lives in Villa Åkerlund; that's in the middle of a public park. Anyone can take a stroll around it, even us."

Petrov paused and waited for Sofiya to join the conversation. She shrugged her shoulders and took another bite that she chewed conscientiously. He kept waiting until she offered, "As I said, I don't need a geography class."

Petrov's hands tensed on the table, but his face remained

under control. "This isn't about geography, Sofiya. It's about the sense of safety the Americans feel. They're not on their guard and easy to approach."

There it was, she thought. *There was someone he wanted her to approach.*

"I've met the American ambassador, and I'm on speaking terms with all the highest-ranking counsellors," Petrov continued. "I wouldn't say that we're friends, far from it, but there's a mutual understanding between us, in this city. Or so we let them believe." He paused to make sure he had her entire attention. "We know the Americans have submarines in the Norwegian Sea and above Finland, ready to deploy and shoot at us. But we don't know where they are, and we can't crack their communications. There's a comm relay in the American embassy; if we could get our hands on their code…"

"TJ–9, I suppose," Sofiya guessed that elusive code was what he'd promised Moscow.

The diplomat nodded. "The weakest link in their ranks is Timothy Johnson, the Minister-Counsellor. With the right kind of leverage, he could be persuaded to let us in."

Sofiya scoffed at the scope of the task at hand. "You want to turn the Minister-Counsellor? You're crazier than I thought."

"Not turn him; that would take more leverage and money than even I can access. With your help, I will only ask him for one small favour."

Petrov sat up and moved to the living room. He motioned for Sofiya to follow him. She obeyed and found him standing next to the coffee table with a briefcase in hand. He opened it and placed it atop the wooden surface. A manila folder, emblazoned with the Soviet Union logo, sat atop the pile. He reached for it before handing it to Sofiya.

Flipping it open, she discovered the picture of a man who had to be between thirty-five and forty years old. He had a kind, round face, deep brown eyes, and a youthful smile.

"Timothy Johnson," Petrov confirmed. "And everything we know about him. Including the nightclubs that he likes to frequent and the hotel he takes his mistresses to."

"What happens when he sees me on your arm at your next cocktail dinner? He'll recognise me for sure."

"Don't worry about that; it's all part of the plan."

It was a plan to which she only knew the outline. From the hard set of the man's jaw, it was obvious he wouldn't give her more information than what was in the file. Her usefulness had its limits, and Sofiya felt like she had just exchanged one master for another. That realisation left a bitter taste to her mouth, and she felt like washing down her sandwich with a glass of vodka or two.

"I know what you're thinking," Petrov broke her musing as he closed the briefcase. "He's using me like the KGB used me. He only sees me as a thing, as sexual bait, nothing more."

"Not that far from the truth, is it?" Sofiya said, letting the bitterness she felt colour her words.

"This mission is important," the diplomat continued, ignoring her interruption. "It will give us a considerable lead over the Americans. We'll be congratulated by the Motherland for what we're about to do."

Sofiya scoffed. "Please give me a break; you're as much a patriot as I am your beloved girlfriend."

"*Fiancée*." Petrov gave her a smile that was as fake as his devotion to the cause. "I think it best to update your status."

Hell, now she really needed that drink. Dropping the

folder on the sofa, she turned on her heel and marched to the liquor cabinet without a single glance at her betrothed. The vodka she found in there was the expensive kind, and she poured herself a large glass.

    Petrov let her have it and left the room without further explanation.

FRIDAY, APRIL 11, 1986.

STOCKHOLM, SWEDEN.

Petrov was silent as he drove his car through the night. They were going north, Sofiya noticed, and soon left the island of Kungsholmen behind. Turning right after Karlbergs Palace, they entered the Vasastan district and followed the river south until they reached *Gamla Stan*—the old town. Situated on the Stadsholmen island, Gamla Stan was known to the locals as *Staden mellan broarna*—the town between bridges. With its medieval alleyways, cobbled streets, and archaic architecture, Gamla Stan was a maze of narrow paths and sharp turns. It was also the home of some of the city's most secret nightclubs.

Petrov stopped the car at a deserted street corner. Pointing at the entrance of a dark alleyway, he said, "Take that road; the club will be on your left."

Sofiya nodded and reached for the coat she had left on the backseat.

"Know what you have to do?" the man asked, his gaze surveying their surroundings.

The young woman nodded again and opened the door. She was halfway out of the car when Petrov's cold fingers wrapped around her wrist.

"I asked you a question, Sofiya," he said, in a tone that commanded an answer.

"I know what is expected of me." She shrugged her arm free and left the car. She closed the door with more force than was necessary.

She shivered in the cold night and wrapped her long coat tighter around herself. The weather here wasn't as cold as Moscow, but that damn humidity had the knack of chilling her to the bone. She hurried to the alleyway and only slowed when pavement gave way to cobblestones. Behind her, she heard Petrov turn the car around and drive away.

She found the club entrance easily. The red neon of its sign glowed vividly in the dark, luring in customers like the wicked sirens of Ancient Greece. She pushed open the door and almost coughed at the smell of stale smoke and sweat that hung inside.

She checked her coat in the locker and used that time to get used to the new surroundings of disco beats and dim lighting.

Tonight, she'd let her long brown hair loose, and wavy strands cascaded on her bare shoulders. The shimmering red sequins of her dress reflected the coloured lights dazzling at various angles. The strapless outfit was very snug, moulding itself to her every curve. Ending mid-thigh, it made her long legs seem even longer. Black pumps with high heels completed the ensemble.

Leaving the locker behind, she tried arranging the front of her dress to make room for her breasts—damn, but she could hardly breathe in this.

There was an animated mass of people, young and old, on the dance floor. Through the loudspeakers, a woman warned that it was going to 'rain men' to an upbeat tune, and the dancing crowd tried to keep up with the rhythm on the dance floor.

Several women wandered around in dresses similar to Sofiya's, but few of them had bodies as attractive as hers. They also lacked the grace with which she moved through the room.

The young Russian pushed forward in search of her prey, and the dancing spotlights made the sequins sparkle on her dress. The women on the dance floor were quick to assess the competition, and she received more than her fair share of jealous glares. The men's ogling stares were more welcoming. Having crossed through the dancing horde, Sofiya found Timothy Johnson leaning against the bar. He was of medium height but with an athletic build, and he wore his dark-brown hair close-cropped. By the looks of it, he'd had several drinks already, and his nose was dangerously close to a blonde's cleavage.

The girl was short-legged and slightly plump. She'd done her makeup in a blunt, obvious fashion and tied her hair in a messy bun. Her looks screamed 'easy lay', and Sofiya wasn't surprised that Johnson had singled her out.

Well, she thought as she aimed for them, *let's see if we can up the offer.*

She chose to come up behind the man, and then walk past them slowly to reach the bar behind the blonde. She swayed her hips to the music as she did but made sure not to look their way.

Reaching her destination, she waved to catch the bartender's attention. It was only then that she let herself turn her head to the side. Acting as if she was merely taking in her surroundings, she met Johnson's gaze over the blonde's shoulder. He had noticed her, and Sofiya smiled inwardly.

She gave him a polite nod and returned her attention to the bartender who was now facing her. She ordered a gin and tonic and drummed the counter to the music beat as she waited. When she looked up, she found Johnson's reflection in the mirror behind the stacks of bottles that faced her. Though he was busy talking to his date, his eyes kept darting back to her.

Once she'd paid for her drink, she brought the tall glass delicately up to her lips before turning to face the dance floor. She met Johnson's gaze once more and held it a little longer this time before re-directing her attention to the dancers.

She leaned back against the counter and placed both elbows on the flat surface. Her breasts pushed forward as she arched her back, and this time, she needed no mirror to know Johnson's eyes were locked on her.

She counted to twenty in her head before taking another sip of her drink. In doing so, she glanced his way for the briefest of instants—almost as if by accident. Having returned her gaze to the crowd, she waited another five seconds before angling her head his way to allow for a more earnest look. He was still looking her way, and this time, she let him know she had noticed him, too.

The blonde woman was talking animatedly now, but it was obvious to anyone but her that Johnson wasn't listening. Sofiya let herself smile mischievously at that, and Johnson returned her grin along with a shrug.

Turning to face him, drink in hand, the young Russian stood behind her competition. She raised her glass and a challenging eyebrow. *Shall I get rid of her?* she silently asked the American. Johnson's smile grew amused, and she poured her glass down the girl's back.

The blonde shrieked in surprise, straightened like she'd just been struck by lightning, and in the mayhem, knocked her own cocktail glass down her lap.

"Oh my god," Sofiya said in flawless Swedish. "Someone elbowed me, and—oh dear, I'm so sorry."

Johnson couldn't help but smile as he handed the poor girl a wad of napkins. She did her best to patch her front but couldn't do anything for her back. She turned a murderous gaze towards Sofiya before excusing herself and heading for the ladies' room.

The young Russian made sure the stool was dry before taking her place.

There was an amused spark in the brown eyes of the man facing her. "You certainly know how to make an entrance," he said.

Sofiya allowed herself a small victorious smile. "Yes, and you owe me a drink."

Johnson pulled out a money clip and handed a few notes to the bartender. Minutes later, the man placed a bottle of champagne and two glasses by their side.

Timothy Johnson had been easy to play. He bought every lie Sofiya fed him without question; he swallowed them hook, line, and sinker, and was all but ready to take a bite of the fisherwoman, too. As Petrov had planned, the Minister-Counsellor offered to take her to a hotel rather than his home. And as luck would have it, he knew the perfect place within walking distance. Sofiya was eager to agree, and she tipsily clung to his arm the whole way as her high heels navigated the treacherous cobblestones.

It was close to midnight when they reached the hotel. Johnson left her to wait in the lobby while he got them a room. Sofiya took the opportunity to fix her makeup in the hallway mirror with a sure hand that neither trembled nor hesitated. The sips of G&T and subsequent glasses of champagne had had little effect on her. She was used to much stronger stuff and had built up quite the tolerance to lighter drinks over the years.

Sofiya and Johnson were in the elevator less than five minutes later, kissing the whole way up. The American started unbuttoning his shirt as they walked down the corridor to their room. He was eager to get between her legs, and Sofiya knew the preliminaries would be short. She kicked off her shoes as soon as she got inside the room, and dropped her coat, which was quickly followed by Johnson's own coat and shirt, on a wooden armchair.

There was nothing ostentatious about the room. A single king-size bed stood in the centre, with two wooden bedside tables on each side. A small wardrobe stood in one corner, next to a door that probably led to the bathroom. A metre from the foot of the bed stood a large window.

The curtains were closed, but Sofiya pushed them open to reveal a partially unobstructed view of Lake Mälaren, and in the distance, the island of Skeppsholmen. The waxing crescent moon's shattered reflection moved with the swells of the lake and chased up the shore with the tide. In the distance, a smattering of house and traffic lights were like beacons on the darkened landscape.

Johnson came to stand behind her, and she angled her head to the side as his mouth moved to her neck. Both of his hands came up to her breasts, and she could feel him harden against her back. She smiled; Petrov's plan was unfolding to perfection.

Johnson had chosen the same hotel he always took his mistresses to, and the night manager Petrov had handsomely paid gave him the room they had agreed upon. As she let her gaze take in the peaceful scenery, Sofiya could make out the contours of the tall building to the side in which Petrov waited, armed with a top-of-the-range, long-lensed camera. By the look of things, he wouldn't be disappointed.

Johnson's moves were getting frantic as he fumbled to free her breasts from the tight dress. The young woman turned in the American's embrace and pulled the small zipper hidden beneath her right armpit down. Without pulling down the twin zipper on the left, Johnson wouldn't be able to fully undress her, but that was enough to free everything down to her stomach. The young man wasted no time doing just that before pushing her back until she was flat against the window.

Sofiya shivered at the cold surface hitting her shoulders, and she moved to undo the American's belt. By the time she got rid of his trousers and underwear, he had a finger in her mouth and one of her nipples between his teeth. Pushing her dress up so that it pooled at her waist, she used one hand to remove her panties and the other to stroke him to full hardness.

Once he was ready, Sofiya spread her legs, and he stopped toying with her breasts long enough to take himself in hand. Penetrating her dry, Johnson did nothing to ease his entrance. The young woman let a sound that was half a scream of pain and half a moan of pleasure escape her throat as he buried himself deeper inside her. He moved back out, almost leaving her completely before thrusting forward again, going deeper still. Sofiya moaned again, and Johnson repeated the action until he couldn't contain himself. The little swallow had played her cards right, and the American was delirious with desire. Out of control, he started fucking her violently, for *that* was the type of man he was, *this* was the kind of sex he desired. And so, she gave it to him, moaning in pleasure even as she allowed the pain that he was causing her to show on her face.

Johnson increased the rhythm with each stroke, and Sofiya feared the window at her back wasn't going to last much longer. Lifting her hips, she pushed up against her lover to allow him to bury himself deeper inside her, even as she relieved some of the strain forced upon the fragile surface behind her.

Sofiya remained in control while Johnson surrendered his body and will to her. Grunting and groaning, he was at her complete mercy, and she relished the thought, feeling more alive at that moment than she had felt the whole week.

Sensing him close to the edge, she brought their lips together. Clenching her pussy, she faked an orgasm, and he exploded deep inside her. Out of breath, he crumbled on her an instant later.

"God, you're good," he whispered in English before slipping out of her.

A contented smile bloomed on his moist lips as he bent down to reach for his discarded clothes. Sofiya gave him back that same satisfied smile as she pulled her dress back up.

Though she was covered in sweat, and her body showed all the signs of having had a great time, the young spy only wanted one thing: to return to Moscow.

SUNDAY, APRIL 13, 1986.

STOCKHOLM, SWEDEN.

At eight, the alarm clock buzzed to life, and Sofiya turned it off with a sigh. Pushing the covers off her, she sat up and wondered where Saturday had gone.

She hadn't seen hide nor hair of her fiancé yesterday. He hadn't been home when a cab deposited her at the building's entrance in the early hours of the morning. She surmised he must have gone to the hotel to recover the listening device he'd planted in the room earlier that day. Dragging herself through the apartment, she nabbed a bottle of vodka from the liquor cabinet and took it with her to the bathroom. She drank straight from the bottle as she waited for the hot water to fill the bath. Half a bottle of soap later, she fell asleep in the tub.

Standing up, Sofiya vaguely remembered waking up at some point and fixing herself a quick lunch before she dragged herself back to bed again.

She moved to the bathroom, desperate to brush her teeth, and found an empty vodka bottle on the flowery floor mat.

Reaching down, she placed it in the bin before turning the faucet and dunking her face under the ice-cold spray.

Despite all the sleep she'd had, she looked like shit. She wasn't twenty anymore, and her bad habits were starting to show. She brushed her teeth, untangled her messy hair, and applied a thick layer of foundation and makeup to her skin. When she entered the living room, it was a quarter to ten, and she now looked radiant.

Viktor Petrov and his fiancé were expected at a garden party at eleven, and she was right on time for the happy couple to make their debut into the Stockholmian social scene.

Petrov parked his car along the alley of a large Manor in Östermalm. Though the clouds hung low in the sky, the sun's thick rays shone through. There was a comfortable spring warmth to that April day that even the light wind coming in from Lake Mälaren couldn't dispel.

A small gathering of smartly dressed men and women pooled out of a dozen cars parked before and after them. The couple followed them to the entrance.

"Ready?" Petrov asked as they arrived at the front gate of the Manor's park.

Sofiya tightened her light-beige coat and nodded. "Of course."

They had rehearsed their story on the way, deciding to keep it as close to the truth as possible to avoid stupid mistakes. Sofiya worked for the government in Moscow; the two had met during his last trip back home. He'd asked her to accompany him to an evening at the Kremlin, and when he'd seen her, waiting shyly by the entrance in that long auburn dress, he'd fallen in love.

The tall wrought-iron gate opened to a large, manicured park. Several flowerbeds dotted the lawn at intervals, swirling left and right. A central gravel path, lined on both sides by symmetrical grooves, led the visitors to the Manor's entrance.

Petrov placed his arm around Sofiya's back, and they stepped onto the gravel path. Under his black coat, the diplomat wore another of his navy suits and an off-white shirt. Sofiya had opted for a long chocolate-coloured dress with a slit down one side. She'd left her hair loose and tried to push some of the bangs to the side with hair gel.

At the Manor's entrance, a red carpet led them to a large reception hall; it was nowhere as big as the Kremlin's, Sofiya noticed, but it was no less stunning. One length of the room was entirely made of large windows that opened to the gardens, while the wall on the opposite side was covered in large paintings depicting various Stockholmian landscapes.

Turning to look on her left, Sofiya noted a large chimney with an intricately carved, gold-plated mantelpiece. The fire in the hearth hadn't been lit; instead, several buffet tables stood in front of the area.

The sun that shone through the windows brought a certain warmth to the atmosphere, and Sofiya noted that two of the glass doors had been left open so the guests could move in and out of the garden. The happy couple mingled with the crowd, offering the guests a twin set of amiable features and relaxed smiles.

A ginger-haired woman in a tight-fitting, low-cut black dress zeroed in on them with an exaggerated smile. "Viktor, so glad you could come," she said in Russian-tinged Swedish.

"How are you, dear?" Svetlana Alexeïeva reached for Petrov's arm before leaning forward to kiss him on both cheeks. In doing so, she managed to put some distance between the young diplomat and his fiancé, and Sofiya couldn't help but wonder if this older woman was subtlety attempting to mark her territory.

Petrov pushed her back a little before turning to Sofiya to make the required introductions. "This is Svetlana Alexeïeva, the Minister-Counsellor of the embassy and my superior."

Sofiya acted as if that was news to her and reached a hand forward, even as she bowed her head politely. "Pleasure to meet you."

Though the Minister-Counsellor was in her fifties, you wouldn't have guessed it—not with the heavy layer of foundation she'd applied on her face and around her almond-shaped brown eyes. Unlike Sofiya's makeup, which gave her a fresh look, Alexeïeva's was too heavy and, therefore, almost vulgar.

The ginger-haired woman shook her hand with a strong grip. "You must be Sofiya," she said, her artificial smile unwavering, "I've heard so much about you."

"Oh, I've heard of you, too," she couldn't help but add. *Let her read whatever she wants into that,* thought Sofiya.

Alexeïeva saw the threat for what it was and replied in kind, turning to Petrov with childlike eagerness. "Oh, Viktor, you will never guess who I ran into earlier."

Sofiya's fiancé, who appeared all but blasé at the girls' antics, merely raised a questioning eyebrow.

"Oh, come on, dear," she purred. "You have to try to guess. No?" Returning her attention to the crowd, Alexeïeva searched the various groups present in the room. When she found who she was looking for, her smile widened. "There," she said, with a nod of her head. "By that large painting of a bridge."

Both newcomers followed her gaze, and Sofiya's heart sunk when she recognised the round face, deep-set brown eyes, and youthful smile. Timothy Johnson, the American diplomat she'd been forced to sleep with two nights before, stood in the middle of a group of on the opposite side of the room.

"Isn't it a small world," crooned the ginger-haired woman, and Sofiya understood that this had been part of the plan—Petrov *and* Alexeïeva's plan—all along, it would seem.

Johnson was busy shaking hands with an elderly couple and didn't notice them until Alexeïeva waved her hand to him to get his attention. He turned a smiling face her way and made his excuse before moving in their direction.

Surprise froze his step when he caught sight of Sofiya. He was quick to recover himself, and a blank mask settled on his features as he reached their group.

"Minister-Counsellor Johnson," purred Alexeïeva as she extended a hand. "How's my American counterpart doing?"

"Very well," Johnson shook her hand and then Petrov's. "Counsellor."

There was a slight hesitation when he came upon Sofiya. She saved him from embarrassment by reaching her hand forward and introducing herself.

"My fiancé," Petrov indicated, as the two shook hands like it was the first time they'd met.

"Oh! Oh, that's—" A slight blush crept in the brown-haired man's cheek as he faltered to finish his sentence. "Oh, congratulations, Counsellor Petrov." He was saved from having to speak further by the arrival of his wife.

Sonia Johnson was a thirty-nine-year-old, short, raspberry blonde woman. Troubled light-blue eyes shone out of her freckled face as she took her husband's arm.

"There you are, Timmy. I thought I'd lost you," she said, relief evident on her emaciated face. Though she'd spent several years in Sweden, her American accent was impossible to miss.

Sofiya regarded her with interest. There hadn't been much information about Mrs Johnson in the file she'd been given. All that she knew was that the two had met in college and gotten married when they were nineteen. A note had also been made of the woman's frail health and subsequent weekly medical appointments, including one with a psychiatrist.

"My wife, Sonia," Johnson said before he introduced her to the three Soviets.

"My fiancé is new to Stockholm," Petrov added at the end of the introduction. "She only arrived last week."

"Oh welcome, dear," Sonia said, sounding sincere. "If you need someone to show you around, let me know."

"Sonia, dear," mumbled an embarrassed Johnson, "Please remember who you're talking to."

His wife seemed upset he'd interrupted her. "The war is over, Timmy. And we're all civilized people. We should behave as such; don't you think?"

"Absolutely," purred Alexeïeva. "There are, after all, certain areas in which our two countries share the same tastes."

The subtext was lost on the frail American woman, but her husband heard it loud and clear. Red tinged his cheeks, and he faked a cough to hide his embarrassment. Sofiya didn't blink, neither did Petrov.

"Darling," said Johnson, putting an arm around his wife's

shoulders. "I need to speak privately with my Soviet counterparts. Would you excuse us, please?"

"Of course," replied Sonia; reaching for Sofiya's hand, she said, "Us girls will keep each other company while you all talk shop."

Sofiya forced a relaxed smile on her face as she was led away by the wife of the man who had mercilessly taken her against a cold hotel room window only two days before. Out of the corner of her eye, she saw Petrov and Alexeïeva head to the entrance door, followed closely by Minister-Counsellor Johnson. The two Soviets wore bright smiles as they left the room, but the American's head hung low. He'd been had; this was not a mere indiscretion he had to keep from his wife—no, the American ambassador's second-in-command had just made the mistake of sleeping with a Soviet diplomat's fiancé. Sofiya had little doubt that the photographs and recordings of what happened in that hotel room were going to be handed to him in one of the Manor's secluded corners, along with an offer of blackmail.

Sonia Johnson led them both to the terrace and onto the gravel path that snaked through the gardens. Though she looked thin and tired beneath her makeup, Sofiya discovered the American was a chatterbox, and she emanated genuine kindness. She was curious to know how her new acquaintance had met Petrov, and she volunteered her own love story once Sofiya was done recounting her made-up fairytale. This lasted them the entire walk through the garden. When they reached the terrace again, Sofiya snagged a champagne glass from a passing waiter. She drank it in one go before reaching for another one.

"Thirsty, are you?" asked Sonia with mirth.

"Sorry, did you want one?" Sofiya asked, realising the waiter was gone.

"No, I can't—not with my medication." The American looked chagrined for an instant before she recovered herself. "You enjoy it for me. But don't throw the glass behind your shoulder when you're done."

"Don't worry," Sofiya chuckled, taking a sip, "We only do that with cheap vodka glasses."

"That reminds me, I wanted to ask you something. Our names are the same, are they not?"

The young Russian thought about it for an instant before nodding. "Yes, Sonia is the common hypocoristic of Sofiya."

That coincidence seemed to delight the American greatly. *Our first name's not all we share*, thought the Soviet spy bitterly as she finished her drink.

TUESDAY, APRIL 15, 1986.

STOCKHOLM, SWEDEN.

Sofiya woke up early and ate breakfast alone.

Her fiancé had already left for work, and she took her plate with her to the living room balcony to enjoy the view as she ate.

Once she was done, she prepared a quick letter to her 'aunt'—one that would assure her that she had made it safely to Stockholm, and all was going well. She chose not to use any of the code-words that would request Serov set up a meeting. She figured it was too early for that, and she had nothing substantial to report anyway. Though she wholeheartedly shared Moscow's opinion of Viktor Petrov, she had nothing incriminating to offer them. His plan to use Timothy Johnson was in line with the *Komitet*'s directives, and his affair with Svetlana Alexeïeva would be of little interest to Directorate K.

As she wrapped up the missive, Sofiya pondered her next move. Since their talk in the alley and Petrov's promise to her of a fresh start, the diplomat hadn't broached the subject again. Ten days she'd been here, and for over ten days, he'd given her little more than discontent and a cold shoulder. The truth was, Sofiya was nowhere closer to figuring him out than when she first met him, and that drove her crazy. Petrov's controlled manners and guarded face gave nothing away—and to think she was normally an expert at understanding what made people tick. All she could do was wait; loath as she was to admit it, the ball was in Petrov's court. Should he decide to hint at wanting to fulfil his promise, she would help him. If not, she'd have no choice but to do what Moscow expected from her—even if it meant throwing him to the wolves.

On her way to Östermalm, she dropped the letter in a box. As she neared her destination, she braced herself for what awaited her. She had plans to spend the day with Sonia Johnson, of all people. The American had apparently taken a liking to her at the garden party and offered to take her for a shopping trip in town. She'd bragged about knowing all the best boutiques, and she apparently couldn't wait to help the newcomer broaden her sense of fashion. Not wanting to appear rude, Sofiya had no choice but to accept the invitation. Besides, she needed to buy some clothes anyway.

Spring was in full bloom in the Scandinavian capital, and Sofiya enjoyed the feeling of sunshine caressing her face. Mingling with the locals, she took the bus to the centre of Östermalm and then made her way to the embassy district on foot. *The embassy district—now there was a joke,* she thought with a wry smile. The Kingdom of Sweden may proclaim its neutrality loud and clear, but it had, nonetheless, made a point to separate the Soviet embassy from its brothers and sisters. While the happy clan of America, Hungary, Turkey, Norway, Germany, Italy, Finland, and Great Britain stood within walking distance of each other in Östermalm, the black sheep of the family had been relegated to a whole other island, some twenty minutes away.

She had no trouble finding the American embassy on Dag Hammarskjölds väg 31. It was another rectangular-shaped grey building that was both imposing and cold—much like the Russian embassy, Sofiya noted. She walked past it and continued towards Nobelparken. She knew the American ambassador enjoyed the luxury of a private house in that park that overlooked Lake Mälaren, but the rest of the embassy staff had been granted the use of large apartments on Linnégatan, a residential street a little further away.

She easily found the building number that Sonia Johnson had given her. Upon her arrival, she announced herself to the doorman, an elderly man with greying hair and a crisp uniform. He invited her to wait in the lobby while he notified the tenants of the penthouse that she had arrived.

When the old man disappeared around the corner of the room, the familiar figure of Timothy Johnson stepped out of the opposite corridor. Without a word, he took Sofiya by the arm and dragged her down the corridor and to the elevator. He almost threw her in before pressing the button to close the doors. He failed to select a floor, and the elevator stayed where it was, trapping the young woman in its small, stuffy, ensconced space.

"What the fuck are you doing here?" Johnson asked. The kindness he'd shown her at the garden party had completely evaporated, and the young woman took a step back.

"This has nothing to do with you," she said, massaging her wrist. "Your wife invited me; she wants us to go shopping. I couldn't say no, not without giving her an explanation."

"You stay away from her," the American said, closing the gap between them again. "And you stay away from me."

"Trust me; I would like nothing more than to do that." Sofiya tried backing away again, but she soon felt the cabin of the elevator push against her back. "I don't like this situation any more than you do."

"Funny…" Johnson took another step forward. When he glanced down at her body, it was easy to guess at his thoughts. "…you seemed to enjoy yourself the other night."

Sofiya couldn't help but notice how their positions echoed the ones they'd had that night, and she felt something creep up deep inside her, which she refused to acknowledge. She had to put an end to this, she realised. In such a tight space and without any weapons at her disposal, she wouldn't be able to fend him off.

"*You* were having the time of your life," she said, her tone scathing. "*I* was on assignment."

Bending to take a long whiff of her perfume, Johnson chuckled. "Some things cannot be faked." With that, he pressed the button to open the doors, and he stepped to the side.

Sofiya was out of the small cabin in no time, feeling his gaze linger on her back the entire length of the corridor. She found Sonia waiting for her in the lobby and acted like she'd been looking for her all along.

The sun was setting when Sofiya returned to the apartment, balancing several shopping bags in her hands. Each one was branded with a different logo on the side, and they contained a variety of skirts, dresses, pants, and blouses that would last her until summer came.

The young woman was surprised to find Petrov nursing a

drink in the living room. He'd opened a new bottle of vodka and placed an empty glass for her on the coffee table. She dropped the bags by the sofa before sitting down and facing him.

Rather than filling the silence, Petrov filled her glass.

Sofiya studied him as she reached for it. He'd taken his suit off already and replaced it with a pair of cotton trousers and a white shirt. Though the white garment reached high at the base of his neck, it wasn't enough to hide the hickey he had on his collarbone. So—he'd been spending time with Svetlana Alexeïeva again. Sofiya chose not to let Petrov know she'd noticed, but she committed the detail to memory.

The silence stretched, and she emptied her glass before pouring herself another one. She was fine with whatever game the diplomat had going; she could do this all night.

"That's to be expected," Petrov said eventually. "After putting up with Sonia Johnson for an entire day."

"She talks a lot," Sofiya confirmed. "Rarely stops."

"Tomorrow morning, I want you to go to the Johnsons' apartment in Östermalm," he continued. "Pretend it's to thank Sonia for the delightful day you've just had, or something."

He reached into his pocket and placed two items on the table. The first was a thick manila envelope, and the second, a little black plastic device. It had a switch on one side and an antenna on the other. "Once you're there, pass this along to her husband, without her seeing it. He'll know what to do with it."

Petrov waited for her to nod before standing up and leaving the room.

Returning her attention to the items that faced her, Sofiya pondered the situation. She recognised a kill switch when she saw one. Once activated, the little black device would momentarily disable all electrical equipment within twenty feet of where it stood. As for the envelope, its content was easy to guess. The young spy would bet all her money that it was a mix of compromising photographs and a copy of her wild night with Johnson on tape.

The only unknown that remained was the location at which the device had to be activated.

WEDNESDAY, APRIL 16, 1986.

STOCKHOLM, SWEDEN.

As she walked down Linnégatan, Sofiya wondered which course of action to take. The compromising envelope and the kill switch were safely tucked out of sight in her large brown leather shoulder bag, and she knew what was expected of her. Drop the parcel and make it clear that Johnson had better follow the instruction Petrov and Alexeïeva had given him. And then make a swift exit.

If only they'd told her more about the plan and where the device was to be used. *The American embassy, for sure,* she thought. But then what? How did they plan to penetrate the heavily guarded offices? A Soviet citizen, even a diplomat, would never make it past the front gate, let alone wander through the upper floors. And yet, she was certain the two lovers had an airtight plan at the ready.

She needed to figure it out. Directorate K and Serov may have agreed to let her go unsupervised for a couple of months, but she knew that it was a privilege that wouldn't last. That sleazy heel would be breathing down her neck soon enough, and when the time came, she had better have something to bait him with.

Reaching the building entrance to the Johnsons' flat, Sofiya offered a polite smile to the doorman before requesting he announce her arrival. The old man led her inside, and she followed him to the reception, where he proceeded to phone the penthouse tenants. Whoever he spoke to on the line cleared her, and the doorman led her to the elevator.

Before the doors closed, he reached a hand inside to press the top-floor button for her. Forcing herself not to think of what had nearly happened in that lift before, Sofiya focused on relaxing her features as the tiny compartment rode up.

When the doors opened on the fifth floor, the young woman stepped into a small corridor with unadorned white walls. Predictably, there was only one door to knock on. She did, and before bringing her hand back down, passed it through her detached hair to give it more volume. She readied her best smile as she waited.

Timothy Johnson opened the door before letting her in without a word. The American was in a foul mood, and it showed. He hadn't shaved that morning, she noticed, and dark stubble haloed the contours of his round face.

Sofiya removed her coat as she crossed the hallway and placed it atop one of the sofas in the luminous living room. Two large white leather sofas stood facing a television. Bookshelves had been installed on either side of the entertainment unit, and they were filled to the brim. On the other end of the room, a piano stood next to a chimney. It was lit, and Sofiya could feel its warmth reach her even from where she stood. Further away, two large glass doors opened onto a roof terrace that was the size of her flat in Moscow.

The corridor she had taken to get here continued on the other end of the room, presumably leading to the bedrooms, while a passage on her right gave way to the kitchen.

Sonia Johnson was nowhere to be seen, and Sofiya sat herself down in one of the sofas uninvited.

"My wife isn't here," Johnson said. "She's left the city to visit a friend and won't be back until Saturday."

The brown-haired man remained at the living room entrance with his arms crossed over his chest. Anger radiated off him in waves.

Determined to stay on top of that exchange, Sofiya leaned back more comfortably. "I know; Sonia mentioned it yesterday." She winked at him. "If anyone asks, say that I'd forgotten about it."

The chatty American had told her everything about her friend Lena who'd been taken ill and her plan to go visit her in Gotland. She'd even told her new best friend that she would take the 8 am train and that her husband had taken the morning off to see her to the station.

Sofiya, who had phoned ahead to let Sonia know she would be calling in on her later that morning, had timed her call to reach the answering machine. She'd left Sonia a message she would never get, but that had ensured her husband would remain in the flat until she arrived.

The American blew air through his nose before taking a couple of steps closer. "What are you here for?"

Reaching for her bag, Sofiya took hold of the items she'd been entrusted with. She placed them both on the glass top of the coffee table. "I trust you know what this is," she said, leaning back against the sofa. "And what to do with it."

Johnson pounced like a snake, reaching the envelope, and

tearing it open. It contained several small photographs, two rolls of negatives, and a cassette tape.

"No need to tell you, I suppose, that it is more than likely Petrov made copies."

The American moved to the fireplace and threw the tape and the negatives in the fire. He kept the small photographs, though, and pushed them in his back pocket.

Kinky, thought Sofiya, allowing the corner of her lips to lift for an instant.

Some of the anger seemed to have evaporated when Johnson returned to the coffee table to pick up the kill switch. As he bent down to retrieve it, he let his gaze wander to the side, taking in the young woman's bare legs.

Sofiya caught his gaze and held it to let him know she'd noticed.

"Nice dress," he said, as if that explained it, before moving to the kitchen. She heard him open and close several cupboards. When he returned, the little black device was nowhere to be seen, and he had two glasses of liquor in his hands.

"A gift," Sofiya uncrossed her legs and spread them a little; the low-cut raspberry gown rose, revealing the lower half of her thighs, "from your wife."

If that was supposed to give the diplomat pause, it did not affect him, and he let his gaze wander higher up when he handed her a glass.

She took it and dipped her lips in the amber liquid, discovering that it was whiskey. Taking a large swallow, she hummed appreciatively when it burned on the way down.

Johnson imitated her, before sitting down on the edge of the coffee table. "You're an interesting woman, Ms Litvinova.

But the company you keep—I'd be careful if I were you. They're extremely dangerous."

She took another swallow and shrugged, "I do what I must."

"Don't we all," Johnson mused. "Comes with the job, I suppose."

He emptied his glass and placed it next to him on the table. When Sofiya had emptied hers, he reached forward to get it, brushing his fingers down the length of her thigh as he did.

The American's lack of subtlety was evident, and Sofiya sat up straighter, pressing both of her legs closed. "Don't you think Petrov has enough on you?"

A dark chuckle escaped the man's throat. "He does, but *I* haven't had enough. I only got a quick taste last time; I want more—seems only fair given the price I'm about to pay for it."

Sofiya frowned at him, curious to know what that price was. "Is that so?" she asked, hoping that he might divulge some of the Soviets' plan.

"I want the rest of you." Johnson used both hands to spread her legs open again. "The real you."

"Don't be stupid; I'll soon be Mrs Petrov," Sofiya said in a sharp tone. "Surely, there are enough doe-eyed secretaries around the American embassy for you to get your weekly quota."

Despite her harsh words, the young woman made no attempt to close her legs, and Johnson let his hands wander higher up.

"There are," he said, "but none of them are as captivating as you."

"And who says I'd be interested?" asked Sofiya, without

acknowledging either the compliment or the man's bold actions.

"You're lost here and alone. I can see that." Johnson's hands reached further up, pushing the raspberry material out of the way. "Who else but a desperate person would want to spend the day with my wife?"

Sofiya scoffed. "You know nothing about me."

"Oh, but I do," he said, his fingers reaching their destination. "Or else, why would you have chosen to wear a dress like this one to come see me." He punctuated his words with a graze of her most sensitive spot, and Sofiya shivered.

She knew she should have stood up and left, knew that giving in to whatever folly this was could cost her life. But Johnson had pushed her panties to the side, and the promise of what was to come had awoken something deep inside her. That feeling of liveliness she'd felt in that hotel room was surging back up, and she wanted more of it.

"Let me know you, Sofiya Litvinova," the American murmured as his fingers sought entrance. "Bodies speak louder than words."

"This could be the death of us," she whispered, spreading her legs further apart.

It was all the invitation Johnson needed. Removing his fingers quickly, he reached for the woman's ankles and pulled until her back was flat on the sofa. Without wasting time, he climbed on top of her and pressed a knee to her stomach. He trapped her under his weight, a sure way to stop her from leaving should she change her mind.

In the whirlwind of motion, Sofiya's left breast escaped the confines of her dress, and Johnson plunged forward to take the erect nipple between his teeth. He bit down hard, while he freed himself from the confines of his trousers and underwear.

The American needn't have worried about entrapping her; the Soviet agent had no intention of leaving anytime soon.

SATURDAY, APRIL 26, 1986.

STOCKHOLM, SWEDEN.

Sofiya had been living in Sweden for only twenty days, but you would never have guessed it. In her hand, she had the latest edition of the *Aftonbladet*—a popular local newspaper. As she rode a bus that crossed through Östermalm, she looked like every other university student out on a stroll. She'd chosen a shrimp-coloured, zip-necked knit top with drop shoulders and a sleek-looking, super stretchy pair of high-waisted denim. She'd gathered her hair up in a ponytail and finished the look with a fake pair of round reading glasses.

She sat up straighter when the bus entered the embassy district, paying attention to the people who climbed in and out at the various stops. From her seat at the back, she had an unobstructed view of the whole bus, and she noticed her target the moment he stepped in. He'd entered by the door closest to the driver and sat down next to a window, in the first half of the bus.

Sofiya got up and came to sit next to him, appearing to

have climbed on board by the rear door. She greeted the man with a polite *"Hej"* before spreading the *Aftonbladet* open wide in her lap. The plump moustached man got off the bus two stations later, excusing himself as he forced the young woman to stand to get out of his seat. She obliged him with a polite smile.

The bus started to move again, and Sofiya allowed herself a glance down at the small rectangular object she now held in her hand. Light reflected off the laminated surface of Richard Starck's ID badge, and she smiled as her gaze settled on the American seal at the top.

She got off at the next stop and found Petrov's car parked on the curb, the engine running. He drove off at high speed the instant she got in.

"Got it?" he asked as he u-turned on a smaller street.

"Of course," Sofiya said, flipping the newspaper open to reveal the ID badge she'd hidden inside.

The car backtracked along the road the bus had taken, entering the embassy district again. Slowing down, Petrov turned into an underground parking station two streets away from the American chancery. He parked his car next to a black delivery van.

The vehicle's back doors opened, and Sofiya climbed in a minute later. Svetlana Alexeïeva was waiting for her inside, ready for a makeover session. Some thirty minutes later, a Richard Starck look-alike climbed out of the van.

"What do you think?" asked Alexeïeva, from where she stood, perched next to the back doors.

Petrov stepped closer to Sofiya, inspecting the result. "Good enough," he replied, and the young woman smiled, stretching the thick moustache that had been glued above her top lip.

"You might end up making me change my mind about her, Viktor," said Alexeïeva as she got out of the van. "I think this broken bird could turn out to be useful to us after all."

Though the comment hadn't been meant for her, Sofiya answered it with a cold, dark stare. She'd have gladly said more, but now was not the time to pick a fight with the ginger-haired Minister-Counsellor.

Without a word, she pinned Starck's ID badge to her breast pocket and rearranged her tie. Beneath the wrinkled brown trousers and checked shirt, she wore a padded suit to hide her curves and give the impression of a fat belly. Alexeïeva had helped her put on a wig and glued a pair of bushy eyebrows and a thick moustache to her skin.

To complete the look, Sofiya had forced wads of cotton in her mouth to round her cheeks and placed brown-coloured lenses over her green pupils. The result was convincing, and from afar, no one would have thought she was a woman.

Though it was only four in the afternoon, the sun had already begun to set when Sofiya reached the security gate.

She feigned a cough as she handed her badge to the guard. "I'll only be a—couple of minutes," she whispered in low tones, keeping the cough going. "I forgot to—fax a report."

The guard nodded before scanning the ID. A green light blinked back at him, and he buzzed the Soviet spy in.

There was only a skeleton crew left in the building, and Sofiya made her way to the third floor without being questioned. Most of the staff didn't work during the weekends, and the few who did, like senior-translator Richard Starck, got to go home early.

Petrov had made her memorise the path to get from the entrance to the ECR, the External Communication Relay office. She reached it with two minutes to spare, and she stopped by a vending machine to not attract any attention while she waited.

Hopefully, she wasn't the only Soviet asset at work in the American embassy, and two floors down, Minister-Counsellor Johnson was busy playing his part. His job was to disrupt the security cameras at precisely 4.15 pm. His instructions were to activate the kill switch and to place it in a paper basket, as close as possible to the security office, before covering it with loose documents. The task accomplished, he was free to return to his daily routine.

The Soviets knew it would take the Americans some time to reboot their systems and even longer to discover the disruptive device. They had calculated that Sofiya had about a ten-minute window.

The ceiling neon lights brightened for an instant, as if experiencing a momentary surge. Sofiya glanced down at her wristwatch and saw that Johnson was right on time.

Checking around to make sure the corridor was empty, she moved to the ECR office and knelt by the door. She pulled a lock-picking tool kit out of her pocket and got to work. Her heart was beating fast in her chest, and she felt the adrenaline surge in her veins. She had the door open in under two minutes—not her personal best, but the fat suit made it harder for her to move.

Slipping inside, she flicked the ceiling lamps on. Sofiya wasn't surprised to discover an austere area with no decoration. On one side of the room stood several tall processors, and on the other, a large desk and several filing cabinets. A personal computer sat on one end of the desk, and a large printer used all the rest of the surface.

The ECR did exactly what it said on the label. The Americans had built dozens of similar offices throughout the globe, each one serving as a relay to safely transmit information to their deployed forces. There were talks of replacing them by satellites in the sky, but the technology wasn't that far advanced yet.

Sofiya sat down at the desk and powered on the IBM workstation. The machine whirred to life, and she pulled a floppy disk out of her pocket. She waited for the operating system to come online to insert it in the slot. She knew these new generation computers could perform up to two million instructions per second with their 40 MB hard drives. As a result, it took less than two minutes for the system to absorb the data contained on the floppy and execute the new commands it required. The printer came to life, and the small print head started moving left to right as the paper unfolded.

With her eyes glued to the door, Sofiya took in a deep, controlled breath. Aware of the time quickly ticking by, she bit her lower lip as she waited for the printer to finish its task. It seemed to take forever, and she used that time to ponder this new development. She'd been surprised when Petrov told her the next step of the plan and what her involvement would be. She had thought he needed her for nothing more than to spread her legs for a man, but she'd been wrong. Or maybe the Soviet diplomat was low on manpower.

So far, the only other ally he seemed to have in Stockholm was Minister-Counsellor Svetlana Alexeïeva, and Sofiya couldn't imagine the obnoxious, prancy woman discreetly breaking into a foreign embassy to start picking locks. Sure, Petrov could have asked Moscow for some help, but Sofiya was dead certain the man preferred keeping everything under his sole control. So, he'd turned to her with an offer she couldn't refuse. A mission like this one—if successful—would wipe more than one black mark from her Directorate K ledger.

It took the printer six minutes to finish its job. Sofiya spent twenty seconds to fold the long sheet of paper. Unbuttoning her dress shirt, she placed it around her fake belly before doing the buttons back up. She was out of the office with one minute to spare, and she used it to lock the door behind her.

There was a bit of a commotion on the ground floor; two guards in uniform stood on each side of the entrance door, and a grey-haired man in a designer suit was animatedly talking to a third guard at the foot of the stairs.

Sofiya ducked her head as she walked past them.

"What are you still doing here, Starck?" the grey-haired man called after her. "I thought you'd gone home already."

Sofiya made sure to take another two or three steps before stopping and turning to face them. There was a large column on her left, and it blocked most of the ceiling lamps. She hoped the distance and the shadows on her face would be enough to sell the lie, for not even her relationship with Minister-Counsellor Johnson would be enough to save her skin if she got caught now.

"Yeah, I'd forgotten to send a fax," she said in a low tone before coughing twice. "S'all good now."

"Sir, the situation at hand?" the officer cut in, drawing the grey-haired man's attention away from the young spy.

"Yes, of course, Lemk," he said, his attention returning to his subordinate. "How long before you can get the system back on?"

Their conversation continued, but Sofiya didn't wait for that man—whom she was fairly certain was the ambassador—to remember she was there. She turned on her heel and was outside the gate within minutes.

Sofiya lost a few of her own eyebrows when the fake ones came off. Her skin itched where the moustache had been glued, and she was glad to be back in her own clothes.

She had made it back to the parking lot without any obstacles. And Alexeïeva had taken the documents from her before leaving in the van she had come with.

Sofiya climbed into Petrov's car, and they drove home.

"What happens to the documents now?" she asked, as they embarked on Ekelundsbron.

"The *Komitet* sent someone from Moscow; Svetlana's going to meet him tonight."

"Do you think the Americans will believe a power surge took down their security equipment?"

"Maybe they'll believe it; maybe they won't," Petrov said, glancing in the rear-view mirror every so often. "It doesn't matter."

It ought to matter, thought Sofiya. "What if they suspect something? The first thing they'll do is change all their codes and protocols, no?"

"Probably, but it'll take them time to coordinate with the

entire float," he explained. "We won't be able to follow their ships for long, but we'll know their position for a short while. And more importantly, we'll know how many there are."

So that was what they'd been after, she thought: *a complete inventory of the deployed American fleet.* While she could certainly see the value that such information could have to Moscow, she wondered if it was truly worth risking two high-ranking Soviet diplomats' careers. Besides, had it been up to her, she would have never used a trump card like Minister-Counsellor Johnson for something so trivial.

Petrov was no fool and must have come to the same conclusions she did. Sure, he was in a tight spot, and the eye of Moscow was upon him, but there were better ways for him to gain a little leeway. That left only one explanation—he hadn't been honest with her and got something more in the bargain.

Now that Sofiya thought about it, she realised she should have seen it coming. Something about Svetlana Alexeïeva had rubbed her the wrong way since day one, and if that crooked diplomat was in on it, it was a safe bet their plan had an ulterior motive.

Try as she might, she couldn't understand the relationship between those two. Alexeïeva was as fiery as Petrov was cold. The annoying redhead craved attention. Wherever she went, she seemed to possess a primal need to be the centre of attention and to be desired by all men present, while Petrov was her polar opposite; discreet by nature, he did his best to stay out of the spotlight. Though it was said that 'opposites attract', Sofiya couldn't fathom what their relationship was like in the privacy of Alexeïeva's bedroom.

As for the information they'd just stolen, well, she wouldn't be surprised to discover the duo kept some of it for themselves; the kind that they could later sell at a good price on the black market.

MONDAY, APRIL 28, 1986.

STOCKHOLM, SWEDEN.

Though the day had started normally enough, Sofiya could never have guessed at how it would unfold and the impact this would have on her future.

After her habitual morning jog and a quick shower, she turned on the local radio as she relaxed in the living room.

Instead of the habitual western music, she caught the end of a special bulletin. "...like we said earlier, there is no need to panic at this stage," a reporter said in a serious tone. "All non-essential personnel have been evacuated as a safety precaution while further tests are being conducted. A representative of the Forsmark Nuclear Power Plant has confirmed that the installation situated north of Stockholm hasn't suffered any visible damage. We will, of course, keep you informed of any further developments."

The special bulletin ended, and the regular programming resumed, with Queen's latest hit, *A Kind of Magic*. Having no idea what this had been about, Sofiya relaxed on the sofa with a fashion magazine in hand.

The phone rang two hours later, and she was surprised to hear Petrov's voice on the line.

"Have you gone out?" he asked her, instead of a greeting.

"For a quick jog," she confirmed, "like every other day. Why?"

"Don't go out again," he said, and she hated how it sounded like an order.

"Why the hell not?"

"Don't be difficult, Sofiya. Just listen to me, will you?"

"I'm not being difficult; you are," she replied. It was one thing for him to control how she ought to dress and which haircut was best for her. But damn, she would not let him dictate how she should spend her free time.

He blew out an exasperated sigh. "Just stay inside, will you? For your safety."

Something in the man's voice told her this was serious, and she was reminded of the special bulletin on the radio. "Is it about what happened at Forsmark?" she asked. "Is it more serious than they said?"

"No, there's nothing wrong with their power plant." Petrov paused, and there was real concern in his voice when he continued, "Look, we don't have all the information yet. I—I'll tell you more when I can, okay? Just, please—stay home, Sofiya."

"Fine, I will," she agreed. "Take care," she added before hanging up the phone—a sign Petrov's concern had unsettled her.

Ever since she'd moved to Stockholm, the man had been on his guard with her. Their conversations had been kept to a minimum, and neither had volunteered anything personal to the other.

Not once had the diplomat given her any impression he

cared about her or her well-being. Rather, he acted as if they were mere colleagues who'd been assigned a task that required two pairs of hands to be completed—until today.

Fearing that something terrible had happened, Sofiya moved to close the balcony door.

Her fears were confirmed when that very evening, the Soviet government issued the following 20-second announcement on the TV news program *Vremya*: "There has been an accident at the Chernobyl Nuclear Power Plant. One of the nuclear reactors was damaged. The effects of the accident are being remedied. Assistance has been provided for any affected people. An investigative commission has been set up."

The habitual programming resumed, and Petrov got up to turn the TV off.

"Is that why the alarms went off at Forsmark?" asked Sofiya, confused.

"It's not just Forsmark," the diplomat confirmed. "There were radiation spikes all over Sweden. They couldn't figure out what it was, so they called their neighbours and discovered it was the same in Finland, Norway, and Denmark."

He returned to sit on the sofa with a worried look on his face. "The ambassador's been juggling phone calls with the Swedish government and Moscow all afternoon."

Sofiya, who hadn't missed the fact that an investigative commission had been created, sat up straighter; they wouldn't do that over nothing. "How bad is it, really?"

"We're not sure yet, but it's worse than what they're letting on." He shrugged. "The Swedes refused to keep quiet about it, so Moscow was forced to make that announcement."

"Should we start stocking up on iodine pills?"

Petrov shook his head. "I've seen the numbers the SSI sent us. They're high, but not that high. There's no cause for alarm just yet."

The *Statens strålskyddsinstitut*, or SSI, was the Swedish National Institute of Radiation Protection and a far trustier source of information than the Soviet Union, thought Sofiya. She knew all about her country's communist propaganda and their habit of twisting the truth until it aligned with the Party's political views.

"Funny they didn't try to pin it on the Americans," she said. "A faulty nuclear submarine, or an unauthorized missile launch, perhaps?"

"There weren't any close by," Petrov indicated. "It's a good thing we gave them that inventory, or else they may well have tried that tactic, only to see it backfire in their face."

Sofiya sat up and walked to the liquor cabinet. She poured herself a glass of vodka and decided to fill another one for her fiancé. "Should I keep staying indoors?" she asked on her way back to the couch.

The diplomat took the drink without thanking her. "The SSI is still compiling data and doing the maths, but they're pretty sure it's safe to go outside."

They emptied their drink in silence, and Sofiya pondered this new change in the situation. The relations between Stockholm and Moscow were already tense, but she feared it would only get worse now. If there was one thing her government didn't tolerate, it was foreigners to try and force their hand. And Sweden had done just that—in a big way.

SUNDAY, MAY 4, 1986.

STOCKHOLM, SWEDEN.

Per request from Petrov, Sofiya had to cancel her plans to meet with Sonia Johnson. And instead of spending her time in more pleasurable company, she found herself seated on Petrov's living room sofa, listening to the diplomat read extracts from an American news article.

"'For people exposed to the heaviest doses of radiation at Chernobyl, death within weeks or months was predicted by public health specialists in Sweden and Italy.'" Petrov paused before resuming further down the paragraph. "'Sweden's radiation protection agency reported that everyone who was within a mile of the reactor might have been exposed to a potentially lethal dose.'"

"This is hardly surprising," Sofiya commented, once it was clear he'd finished reading. "It's what usually happens after a nuclear explosion."

"That's not the point." Petrov threw the paper on the coffee table with more strength than was necessary. "This is."

"The New York Times?" she asked, referring to the item in question.

"The Americans wrote that yesterday, but it's the same everywhere in Europe." He heaved a deep sigh. "Moscow wants this to stop. Yes, there's been a catastrophe; we've admitted to it. Now we don't need everyone looking over our shoulder and judging how we choose to deal with it."

Sweeping it all under the rug, as usual, she thought. "Fine, what's that got to do with us?" she demanded. "I'm guessing you're not bringing this—" she gestured at the paper, "—up for the sake of conversation."

"Indeed not," he said. "Moscow is sending someone to oversee the problem. General Ilia Igorov—1st Main Directorate."

Sofiya sat up straighter. "FCD? But that's External Intelligence." She'd expected someone from Public Relations or Government Communications, not her own main department—and especially not one of the highest-ranking operatives like Igorov. Though the General wasn't Directorate K, his name was well known throughout the service. A veteran of the Great Patriotic War, he had taken part in Operation Uranus in 1942, successfully trapping three hundred thousand Axis troops behind Red Army lines at Kalach. And in November 1943, he was part of the regiments who took Kyiv, earning himself a medal when he was wounded in action.

But more than his acts of war, the man was known for his sharp mind and cunning tactics. Sofiya guessed his involvement in this issue showed how much attention Moscow devoted to the matter.

"His plane took off from Moscow this morning; he'll be here in a matter of hours. All senior staff are expected at the embassy this afternoon for a special meeting."

Sofiya nodded, certain the man would arrive with an

airtight plan to pull all the necessary strings to put Sweden back in its place discreetly. What was more interesting, however, was how unsettled Petrov seemed to be at the FCD general's imminent arrival. She wondered if it was the prospect of someone new bossing embassy employees around that rattled him. Or was it was the fear of having someone as sharp as Igorov snooping into his private business?

MONDAY, MAY 5, 1986.

STOCKHOLM, SWEDEN.

Decorated General Ilia Igorov hadn't disappointed. True to his reputation, he'd come prepared with a plan—several plans, actually. But Sofiya had been surprised to learn, late last night, that one of them involved her.

Once she'd recovered from the news, it wasn't hard for her to make the connections and understand that as FCD himself, Igorov had been informed of the presence of a Directorate K agent in Stockholm—and that being the man he was, the general had sought to put her skills to good use right away.

Thus, Sofiya found herself donning a long blonde wig with wavy curls over a snug black turtleneck. Knowing she'd have a lot of walking around to do today, she put on a pair of white sneakers and a tight-fitting, light-blue pair of high-waisted denim.

The Swedish office of *Credit Suisse International* on Norrmalmstorg 12 was easy to find. Niched between jewellery shops and haute-couture boutiques, the Swiss bank had a welcoming front window that betrayed a lavish interior.

Sofiya used her alias of Malin Waldenström once more to open a secure bank account with the company. It was a brisk affair, and she was surprised at how little paperwork was involved. But then again, she had a little over fifty million Swedish kronor in cash with her that she wished to deposit in her brand-new account, so the bank director proved to be swiftly efficient. She left within an hour with an account number written on a sheet of stationery and a lengthy password that she'd had to memorize in the director's office.

It was a good thing she had a brilliant memory, for she didn't think the FCD would appreciate her losing their money.

Her next stop was south of Norrmalm, on the island of Helgeandsholmen. One of the smallest islands of Stockholm, it housed the Parliament House of Sweden—the Riksdagshuset. The building complex—consisting of a large rectangular ornate stone building on the east and a semi-circular one on the west—took up nearly half the island. What was left of the small body of ground of Helgeandsholmen was covered in trees and manicured lawns.

Sofiya took the western bridge to access the island, and then the circular footpath that surrounded the semi-circular building; then, she walked the width of the eastern building before stopping in the park. She chose the second bench that faced the Riksdagshuset's entrance as she waited for her contact to arrive.

At precisely five minutes to noon, a nervous man in a business suit came to sit next to her. Sofiya briefly glanced his way and saw that he was sweating profusely despite the fresh breeze blowing in from the lake.

"Relax, man," she said in flawless Swedish. "You look like a teenager who just bought his first porn magazine and is carrying it tucked beneath his shirt."

"Easy for you to say," the young man replied, in a voice barely louder than a whisper.

Sofiya had no idea who the kid was; all that she'd been told was the contact protocol and time of the appointment. She guessed the twenty-something athletic blonde was someone's assistant or a trainee of some kind. Either way, this was his very first time making contact with a Soviet agent, and it showed.

"Fine-looking day," she said, using the coded phrase that would identify her. "I fancy going for a boat ride."

"My uncle owns a kayak company," the man replied, his voice stuttering over his excitement. "I could give you his telephone number."

"That won't be necessary," Sofiya said, glancing his way again. If anything, the kid now looked worse than before. He sat at the edge of the bench, with his back ramrod straight, and he looked like he was ready to bolt any second now.

"Would you chill out?" she cautioned. "Anyone looking at you would think you're sitting on a hot plate. Lean back a little; relax your shoulders."

"Have you got my money?" he asked, still in that same nervous, hushed tone.

Sofiya patted her handbag before turning her head to the side, seemingly to appreciate the view. Her posture was the opposite of the nervous wannabe-spy. Her back rested against the bench in a natural and relaxed way. She'd crossed her right leg over the left and had one of her hands delicately poised over her right knee, while the other lay on the bench. A soft smile played at the corner of her lips as she basked in the midday sun. The first rule of such exchanges was to look like you had every reason to be here.

It took the young man a couple of minutes to comply with her directives, but he finally managed to relax a fraction.

"Have you got information for us?" she asked after his back touched the bench, and his left foot stopped nervously beating the pavement.

"Yes, I know how you can get to him. He will attend an art opening on Friday," he explained as he reached for something in his pocket. "I have all the details here."

"Don't take it out of your pocket," Sofiya said, a little louder than was necessary to make sure he'd get the message. Damn, this kid really had no idea what he was doing. "You can't just hand it to me in plain sight."

The nervous foot-tapping resumed as she let out a resigned sigh. "Here's what you'll do. Put your hand in your front pocket, grab whatever piece of paper you have in there —and I hope it's small—then place it against your palm and hold it with your thumb so that it remains hidden."

Without needing to look, Sofiya felt him follow her orders. "Next, you're going to take your hand out of your pocket and slide it down the length of your pants. Now bend down as if you were going to re-tie your shoelaces." The young man did as he was told. "Place the piece of paper beneath your foot and redo your laces before sitting back up."

She uncrossed her legs as she prepared to stand. "See the newspaper on the bench between us? Your envelope is in there." Before the young man had time to ask her questions, she said, "I want you to take it and walk away. Don't worry about the note; don't look back."

A nervous hand entered her field of vision, and she tightened her grip on the straps of her handbag. She stood up half an instant after the man, and when his feet liberated the folded document, she stepped on it herself. Then she glanced down at her watch while the young Swede disappeared back into the Riksdagshuset. Crouching down, Sofiya placed her handbag on the ground as she pretended to look for something inside it. She pulled a tissue out of it with her left hand while she used her right one to discreetly drop the piece of paper inside.

Sofiya had one more task to accomplish for the FCD that day, and that one saw her heading to a less savoury part of town. In northeast Stockholm, she used the last of the money that had been given to her to buy some under-the-counter surveillance material.

The afternoon was nearly over when she entered the flat on Marieberg. She'd expected to find it empty and was surprised to find that Petrov was already home, and he wasn't alone. A man with silver hair and a crisp uniform stood leaning on a cane in the corner of the living room. She froze for an instant before recovering herself.

"General Igorov," she saluted as she entered the living room.

"Comrade Litvinova," he said in Russian. "I trust the day went well."

She nodded. "Of course." She stopped by the coffee table and placed the paper bag that contained the surveillance equipment on the wooden surface. Then she pulled the bank account information and the note she had received outside Parliament House out of her handbag.

Igorov gave it only the briefest of glances. "The password?" he asked.

Sofiya knelt down, found a pencil at the bottom of her bag, and scribbled the ten-digit code on the bank's stationery.

"Good girl," he said. "You Directorate-K operatives are ever so helpful."

Sofiya took no pride in the comment; rather, it ruffled her feathers. There had been something to the man's tone that made the hair on the back of her neck stand on edge. She felt uneasy when she turned her back to him to get to the liquor cabinet. She poured them three glasses of Petrov's expensive vodka and served both men before serving herself.

Both accepted the drinks, though neither thanked her.

"You know what to do with all that," Igorov said to the other man. "There should be enough money in that account to last the embassy for several years. The rest is to be used immediately. The sooner we can get all this mess behind us, the better."

The moment his glass was empty, he left it on the coffee table and bid Petrov goodbye. Sofiya was surprised when he requested that she accompany him to his car.

"I know who you are," the general said once they'd reached the parking lot. "And what your mission here is."

Sofiya wasn't sure if an answer was expected of her, but she gave him one anyway. "I hope this new turn of events won't jeopardize my mission."

"If you're as good as they say you are, you need not worry." He stepped closer to her, his cane tapping the ground in step with his prosthetic leg. "I am not sure I fully understand what arrangement Petrov thinks he has with you, or you with him for that matter. But I have more pressing matters to attend." Coming closer still, he added, "And that includes another mission for you this week."

"A mission?"

"Petrov will fill you in on that." His gaze glanced down and then back up the length of her body as if he were undressing her in his head. "Once that is done, we'll see… I may have other needs for your special kind of services."

His tone, more than his words, had made it perfectly clear what he had in mind.

General or not, Sofiya levelled him with a cold stare as she replied, "I'm an FCD agent, not a prostitute."

A sneer that was full of contempt stretched the man's lips, and he reached a hand forward to grab at her right breast. Blood rushed through Sofiya's cheeks as an impulse to punch him thrummed through her entire body. Reality checked in just in time to remind her that she was nothing more than a field agent and that Igorov was a high-ranking officer and war hero. The hand on her breast tightened before letting go.

"Really?" he said. "You could have fooled me."

With that, he was gone, climbing into the back of a sleek black car that hadn't been there when Sofiya entered the flat earlier. She swallowed hard as she watched it disappear at the end of the street.

She had better pray the current situation would keep the general too busy for any kind of distraction, or else she'd have a hard time telling him no if he ordered her to come and see him for a private meeting.

High-ranking officers taking advantage of subordinates, though illegal, wasn't unheard of within the ranks of the KGB. And such situations were especially frequent with

Department K agents. Sofiya had always managed to evade cases like this, but she'd heard the rumours, same as anyone else. And she knew that if it were to befall her, there'd be nothing she could do about it. Taking the matter to court would only result in a nasty game of 'he said/she said,' and women were well known to lose at that game very often.

Bloody hell, she needed out of this life—like yesterday.

FRIDAY, MAY 9, 1986.

STOCKHOLM, SWEDEN.

Sofiya had never been to the island of Södermalm before. The southern district of the same name was said to be the home of bohemian, alternative culture and a broad range of cultural amenities, and she had to agree with that statement. On her way down the street, she'd walked by two record stores—one that blasted Jamaican music and one that offered more of a Latino vibe—and she now stood in front of a glitzy afro hair salon.

Though it was nearly four in the afternoon, the sun was still high in the sky. A soft breeze blew in from the lake, but it wasn't enough to force her into a coat. Sofiya stopped for an instant to enjoy the feel of the sun and fresh air on her bare legs before turning her back on the small boutique. Then she crossed the cobbled street and entered the art gallery on the other side.

A welcoming, open concept entrance showcasing a few signature pieces greeted her past the door. Further inside, she found a sparse reception desk and plain white walls that ensured the visitors' focus remained on the art. Strategic lighting and room dividers encouraged patrons to wander through the space, and Sofiya counted a dozen men and women spread about the gallery.

The art currently exhibited was from a local artist who was—according to the pamphlet Petrov had given her—modern, audacious, and a worthy successor to the likes of Warhol, Lichtenstein, and Haring. Though she had no idea who these artists were, Sofiya liked the canvases on display—with their provocative metaphors and neon-bright colours.

The upscale crowd attending the showing flowed around her, filling the air with expensive perfumes, and their murmured words of appreciation for the art on display. Sofiya rearranged her hair before joining the ebb and flow. She had parted her long brown strands in two and tied them in twin pigtails with pink ribbons. Both rested on the front of her thin cotton-white blouse to help perfect the schoolgirl outfit she'd been going for. She wore a low-cut, checked skirt and a pair of knee-length white socks in polished black shoes.

The crowd of art enthusiasts might wonder what a teen like her did at an art show, but a second glance at the woman's shapely hips and well-developed breasts would reveal that she wasn't all that young after all. A closer inspection would uncover that she was bra-less and that, in the right light, her white blouse was rather see-through.

It took the young spy little time to identify her mark, and she zeroed in on him like a missile on a target: Erik Nilsson, cabinet member, and *Speaker of the Riksdag*. Holding the second-highest-ranking public position in Sweden, in terms of protocol, after the Monarch, Nilsson was the head and presiding officer of the national legislature and the supreme decision-making body of Sweden, the *Riksdag*.

Currently, the unassuming politician was busy staring at a portrait of a naked woman's torso. The fifty-two-year-old man had a round face and a thick nose. There were tufts of grey hair on either side of his head, but the ones on top had long since pulled a vanishing act. A painting stood in front of his plump belly, and Sofiya feigned interest in it as she moved closer.

"Kinky," she said with a girly giggle. "But I love his use of colours. That vibrant red really highlights her curves, doesn't it? But I wonder what those neon cyan splashes over her torso are supposed to represent?"

"Well yes, it's a nice piece. As for the—uh—the splashes, they—uh," Nilsson's face turned red as he struggled to finish his sentence. "Well—the artist's—uh—*content* perhaps?"

That was a rather mild way of putting it, thought Sofiya. But she acted as if the truth hadn't been staring her in the face the whole time and she'd just now understood what the myriad of dots on the woman's breasts represented. She gaped and brought a hand up to hide her mouth.

"Oh my," she said, with a nervous giggle. "Do you think that it's his—?" she giggled some more, acting as if she was too prudish to say the word 'sperm' out loud.

"I rather think so, yes," said a very flustered Nilsson. "Modern art, you know. It's very daring."

She reached a hand to him and offered him a smile that was all teeth and dimples. "Malin Waldenström."

Turning to face her, the elder man shook her hand with a warm smile of his own. His eyes settled on her face as he introduced himself, and then lowered to take in the rest of her.

Sofiya had positioned herself to catch some of the lights aimed at the painting, and her white blouse had become but a thin veil over her naked skin. Nilsson had obviously found something more interesting than paintings to look at, and though he seemed to make an effort to try and focus on the woman's face, his eyes kept darting down every few seconds.

"Do you like art, Erik?" Sofiya asked, batting her eyelashes at him. "I love it myself."

"Oh yes," he replied, "I love looking at nice things." His gaze darted down once more, making it obvious what he thought was 'nice' in that moment, butced the young spy pretended not to have caught the innuendo. She pushed her shoulders back and arched her back, and her nipples pressed against the thin material.

"I'm a sculptor myself," she said, bringing both of her hands up, fingers wriggling. "I love working with my hands."

There was a catch in the man's voice when he said, "I'm sure you're—uh, very good."

Sofiya kept moving her fingers up and down, as if she were trying to create something out of thin air. Her voice had a husky quality to it when she explained, "It's all about how much pressure you apply, you know? It can't be too much, and it can't be too little. Finding the right balance, that's the difficult part."

Erik Nilsson nodded with a faraway look on his face. Sofiya could easily guess at what the politician had in mind, and *what* he wanted her hands to apply pressure to. She played into his fantasy and started moving her hands more suggestively, cupping and jerking thin air.

Middle-aged men like Nilsson were easy to figure out, and the outfit itself would probably have been enough to lure him to the restroom. But Sofiya was a perfectionist, and she made sure there was no room left in his brain for anything other than sex before she took his arm to guide him to the back of the gallery. She pushed him into the men's restroom, and his eyes grew comically wide when he found himself face-to-face with Petrov's cold, calculating eyes.

The Soviet diplomat had his arms crossed over his dark turtleneck sweater, and his pistol was on full display in his shoulder holster. He was leaning against the tiled wall, and he stayed where he was while the couple entered the tight space.

"Um, I—uh," the Swede stammered as his brain tried and failed to come up with an explanation for the young woman at his arm.

Sofiya saved him from the bother. Closing the door behind her, she let go of his arm and came to stand next to her fiancé.

"Out of respect for your position, Mr Nilsson, we won't take this any further," Petrov said without trying to hide his Russian accent. "And anyway, I think the pictures we took of you in the art gallery with your nose down my friend's shirt, and the ones we have of the two of you entering this room are more than enough, don't you think?"

Nilsson became livid as his dreams of a good time evaporated, and reality returned to figuratively kick him in the balls. "Wha—what do you want?"

"We need Sweden to back off," Petrov explained. "The SSI is officially done meddling in our affairs."

It took a little while for the elderly man to work things out. "What? The SSI— Chernobyl? Is this what this is about?"

The Soviet diplomat nodded, and he moved closer to the politician. The balding man took a step back, and that made Sofiya smile.

"We haven't lied; the numbers we reported are the truth,"

Nilsson started defending himself. "It can't just be a little accident, not with so much radiation reaching our coasts."

Petrov's voice darkened, and the r's became thicker on his tongue, like that of a James Bond villain. "What happened in the Republic of Ukraine is none of your concern, Comrade Nilsson. Moscow will handle this crisis as it sees fit. Now stop feeding the world's paranoia mill."

"If you don't want to have to go through divorce number three, I suggest you do what the man says," added Sofiya, with a pout of her rosy lips.

"Shame on you!" Nilsson said, with a cold stare aimed at the woman. But resignation could be read on his face, and she knew he would do what had been asked of him. "Both of you."

"And a good day to you too," Petrov said, placing his hand at the small of Sofiya's back as he escorted her out.

"That was almost too easy," Sofiya said as they reached their apartment in Marieberg.

"Would you have rather spread your legs for him?" questioned Petrov, as he unlocked the front door.

The question felt like an insult, and she was pretty sure he had meant it as one. "Of course not! I only meant he was an easy mark," she said, almost adding, *not all men keep as close a lid on their emotions as you do.*

"It needed to be done," Petrov said. "All of Europe trembles in fear, and they're pointing their fingers at Moscow, demanding explanations and wondering what truth is being kept from them. It must stop."

Sofiya knew the Motherland was trying hard to keep

Europe's prying nose out of its business, as it dealt with an unprecedented crisis. But the USSR had never been known for its political transparency, and she, too, wondered what was being kept off the news.

"Nilsson wasn't wrong, though; was he?" Sofiya asked, cautiously. "They evacuated hundreds of thousands of people. They wouldn't have done that over nothing."

Petrov remained silent as he moved to the liquor cabinet. He poured himself a glass before moving to sit on the sofa. He'd left the cabinet and the vodka bottle open, and Sofiya moved in to pour herself a large glass.

"How long will General Igorov stay in Stockholm?" she asked. Her real question was, 'how many more missions will I have to do for that pig?', but she chose to be polite about it.

"He's leaving tomorrow," Petrov said, and Sofiya relaxed a fraction. "This was the last part of his plan to put Sweden back in its place." He took a long sip of his drink. "Hopefully, it'll be enough; if not, Igorov will be back for phase two."

And we would not want that, would we? thought Sofiya bitterly. Now that they'd dealt with one crisis, maybe it was time for them to get back on schedule and work at freeing her from the clutches of the Motherland.

"What about Chernobyl?" she asked instead. "How bad is it really, for the people who live there?"

Sofiya moved to sit facing him, on the coffee table. She still wore her thin white blouse and checked skirt, but the pigtails were gone, and now, loose brown waves cascaded freely over her shoulders. Sofiya could have tried spreading her legs to get Petrov to talk, but she knew that would be a waste of her time. She did push her shoulders back a little so that her nipples showed through the blouse again.

The gesture didn't go unnoticed, and the diplomat made a

point to only look at her face as he said, "It will take them months, if not years, to clean up the radioactive waste. A lot of people will lose their lives over that. That's all I know."

Sofiya sighed before taking a long sip of her vodka. "This is bad, isn't it? For the Soviet Union, I mean."

Petrov nodded before finishing his glass. He remained silent, his icy blue eyes locked on hers. The man's expression betrayed nothing of his thoughts, and she looked away.

She instead gazed out the window on her left and to the horizon that stretched on the other side. She looked past Lake Mälaren and its islands, to the East and what lay beyond. The Cold War between her country and the West had been going on for over forty years, longer than she'd been alive. But never had the USSR faced a disaster like this one. The resettlements, the cleaning up—all of that would weaken an already ailing economy. But the true test was going to be the Kremlin's loyal supporters' reactions to how the Communist Party chose to deal with the crisis. In the privacy of her own thoughts, Sofiya feared Chernobyl could be the event that tipped the scale and hastened the decline of the Soviet Union.

Emptying her glass, she muttered, "All wars must end, I suppose."

FRIDAY, JUNE 6, 1986.

STOCKHOLM, SWEDEN.

The festivities of *Sveriges nationaldagh*—Sweden's national day, were in full swing when Sofiya left the Marieberg flat. She had planned on joining the celebrations at Kungsträdgården, one of the city's largest and most central parks.

It was a warm Friday, and she chose to walk rather than take the bus. Turning left, she crossed through Rålambshovsparken and continued east on Norr Mälarstrand. The mile-long street followed the waterfront, and Sofiya let her gaze wander over the glistening waters of Lake Mälaren.

She passed a group of teenagers seated on a bench and heard them humming the country's national anthem, *"Du gamla, du fria."* The two youngest had their cheeks painted blue and yellow, while the other four wore matching shirts with the national flag painted on them.

This surge of patriotism made Sofiya feel oddly nostalgic; it reminded her of Moscow and the communist propaganda that was pinned to the walls throughout most streets. She had never thought she would come to miss the colourful posters designed to encourage the enthusiasm of working masses, but she did. Her childhood had been lulled by propaganda featuring either Vietnam, the space race, or imperialism. More recently, she'd seen the focus shift towards economic restructuring, defeating bureaucracy and Stalinist reactionaries, and her personal favourite: the Party's ongoing battle against alcoholism. There was one image that never failed to bring a smile to her lips; it had a baby girl on the right, a bottle of vodka on the left, and the words "either, or" written in the middle. Only the colour-balance was off, and the little child, with her rosy cheeks and full red lips, looked like she was the one who'd had one drink too many.

When she reached the end of Norr Mälarstrand, Sofiya turned north to head for Stadshusbron, the bridge that would allow her to hop to the next island. From there, it would be a short five-minute walk to Kungsträdgården. Leaving the road, she took a shortcut and entered a small alleyway between two tall buildings. She was halfway through when she felt the presence of a man at her back. It could have been another Swede on his way to the festivities, but she wasn't taking any chances. She hastened her steps, even as she readied to fight.

She'd almost gotten to the other end of the alley when cold fingers encircled her right wrist to halt her. Using her momentum, she turned on her heel. Raising her free arm, she closed her fist and punched the assailant with all the strength she had. She clocked him square in the jaw, eliciting a loud curse in Russian.

Stepping back in surprise, Mikhaïl Serov let go of her arm to bring a hand up to massage his tender jaw.

Sofiya had been ready to follow her punch with a kick to

the guts, but she relaxed when she recognised him. "What are you doing here?"

"Is that any way to greet an old friend?" asked her liaison officer before spitting out a mix of saliva and blood. "Did you have to hit me that hard?"

If he expected an apology, he was bang out of luck, thought Sofiya, as she crossed her arms on her chest. "Most people say hi when they run into someone they know." She had no idea where this conversation was going, but she was already pissed off. "They don't try and grab you from behind."

"Point taken," Serov said, pushing both of his hands into his denim pockets with a half shrug.

He had cut his dark-brown hair shorter, Sofiya noted, and that seemed to accentuate his sharp crow-like features even more. His dark, beady eyes moved quickly left and right as he took in her appearance.

"You look nice in that westerner dress," he said, complimenting the light-green, flowery summer dress she wore. "Lost some weight, too, have you?"

"What do you want, Comrade Serov?" asked Sofiya, putting an end to the pleasantries.

Feigning mock hurt, he said, "It's been two months, and not a word from you. I was getting worried."

Sofiya was in no mood to play. "It's what we agreed on," she reminded him tersely.

"Ah, yes, it is." Serov sighed, and his face lost all traces of humour. "Status update?"

"It's going well," Sofiya lied. "I don't think Petrov suspects anything."

"Noticed anything of interest to Moscow?" he asked.

"I took part in the JT–9 operation, which was successful. I believe the *Komitet* got what it wanted." Serov nodded, and Sofiya continued. "I am not aware of any other mission. But everything else I have seen or heard only proves Petrov's loyalty to the Party. I have no evidence that—"

In the distance, Sofiya heard the familiar opening lines of *"Du gamla, du fria,"* and she paused mid-sentence. Looking up, past the shorter man's shoulder, she noticed the group of boys she'd walked past had just entered the alley.

Serov was quick to react. Reaching up with both hands, he pushed Sofiya back until she was flat against the wall. Taking advantage of her surprise, he pressed his lips to hers with eagerness. While any other man in their situation would have kept it at that until the coast cleared, Serov seized the opportunity to force his tongue inside her mouth, even as he tried parting her legs with his knee. With her arms still crossed over her chest, the young woman was powerless to stop him.

As they walked by, some of the boys snickered and whistled at them while the others kept singing.

The instant the group turned the corner at the end of the alley, Sofiya bit Serov's tongue and stomped his foot with the tip of her heel. Her liaison officer backed off with a howl of pain.

Blood mixed with saliva again, and he spat out once more. "Was that necessary?"

With a cold, dark stare, Sofiya moved to stand in the middle of the alley and well out of Serov's reach. "As I was saying, I think Petrov is clean."

"Why do you protect him? Is it because you like him?" he chuckled. "We know he is having an affair with Svetlana Alexeïeva."

Without missing a beat, Sofiya said, "I know that. But you asked about the man's loyalties, not his sex partners."

"You must not satisfy him completely if he still needs other 'sex partners,'" Serov said. "I hope you're not getting lazy in your old age, little bird."

Sofiya felt like punching him again, but she reined it in. "I haven't tried getting between them," she explained. "I don't trust Alexeïeva—something doesn't sit right with me about that woman. And I think she may try to use Petrov to fulfil her own schemes."

"Ah, so you're using your fiancé to get to her—very good." Serov reached for something in his back pocket. An instant later, he threw a small plastic box in her hands. "Standard listening devices. Place one in her office. I want to know what those two lovebirds talk about behind closed doors."

Sofiya dropped the box in her shoulder bag with a nod. "Anything else?"

"That'll be all for now, but I'll be in touch." At her curious look, he continued. "We can meet in the park when you go out for a run. Stop at the bench, east of the amphitheatre. I'll hide in the bushes on the other side of the path." He paused an instant. "Twice a week ought to do it—so Tuesdays and Thursdays."

With that, Serov left her. He pushed his hands back in his pockets and relaxed his shoulders. He was dressed casually, and nothing was striking about him. As he disappeared down the alley, he looked like any other Swede out on a stroll.

Sofiya waited a full minute before retracing her steps and exiting the alley the way she'd entered. Serov had revealed that he knew her habits—knew where she liked to run and when. Damn, she hadn't noticed him watching her, and now, she wondered what else she had missed—and what else that sleazy heel knew.

Her plans for the day and *Sveriges nationaldagh*'s festivities no longer held any interest for her. Right now, what she needed was mouthwash, a hot shower, and a double dose of vodka.

SUNDAY, JUNE 8, 1986.

STOCKHOLM, SWEDEN.

The American Minister-Counsellor's wife and the Russian Counsellor's fiancé enjoyed a hearty breakfast on the Johnsons' terrace rooftop. As always, Sonia commandeered the conversation and seemed delighted to have found such a pleasant audience. Theirs was the most incongruous of friendships, but both women had agreed that, so long as they stayed clear of politics and their partners' jobs, they weren't doing anything wrong.

Petrov had asked if the good-natured woman could be turned and used to serve the Soviets' agendas, but Sofiya had been quick to dispel the idea. Sonia Johnson was naive to a fault, couldn't harm a fly, and wouldn't be able to tell a lie to save her life.

"She'd probably faint before she got to the end of the first sentence," Sofiya told him.

"Then why continue this masquerade?" asked the Russian diplomat.

"Because I like her." A curious eyebrow rose at that. "Yes, she's dull and naive, and everything else you may think of her. But—she's also the only person I know who is honest with me. It's refreshing."

"Very well, then—keep your eyes and ears peeled, and if you ever get a chance to enter her husband's home office, don't hesitate."

Thus, the weekly encounters had been allowed to continue, and both women met every Sunday at nine for breakfast, which usually lasted two hours. Then, they took a short break while Mrs Johnson excused herself, attending mass at a nearby church. Afterwards, they continued talking long into the afternoon.

For a while, Sofiya had wondered what Timothy Johnson found in this conservative, puritan, woman—his opposite in many ways. Then she'd learned the size of Sonia's bank account, and things started to make sense. Sonia's father had owned a large insurance company in New York, and when he died, some thirteen years ago, everything was split between his two daughters.

Sofiya helped herself to another glass of orange juice, regretting the absence of coffee. Ever since the Chernobyl accident, her hostess refused to ingest anything dairy. And since she couldn't stand her coffee black, she had simply forgone the drink.

Sofiya hadn't been surprised to discover that Sonia had hypochondriac tendencies on top of all her other ailments, which included asthma and allergies to a dozen things. Thus, every week, she listened with an amused smile to the new recommendations the American followed. Chernobyl had added another layer to her health concerns.

When Sweden's National Food Administration recommended that cows should not be allowed to graze outdoors until a region was cleared, based on grass sample measurements, Sonia Johnson had stopped ingesting anything remotely dairy. Never mind that, after closer inspection, half the farms could let their animals loose again.

When the inhabitants of severely hit regions were recommended to refrain from eating green vegetables, such as parsley, chives, dandelions, and nettles, as well as morels, Sonia Johnson became even more selective with her shopping list. The fact that Stockholm was in one of the areas that had received the lowest level of radiation never factored in her equation.

Today, it would seem her latest preoccupation was about eating contaminated fish. "The particles hung in the air and got carried away like clouds, you see," she cited from an article she'd just read, "and when it rained, they fell down. They got into the rivers and the lakes. And I mean, Lord help me, have you seen how many rivers and lakes they have around here?"

"It should help to dilute the particles, no?" asked Sofiya, "I mean, the more water you have, the better."

Sonia considered her statement before saying what she invariably said when she was about to ban a new foodstuff. "I'm not risking it."

Keep that up, and you'll end up eating rice at every meal, thought Sofiya, *and you'll eat it raw because you won't dare touch tap water anymore.*

"Oh my; look at the time," said Sonia, interrupting her train of thought. "Time flies, doesn't it?"

Glancing at her watch, Sofiya nodded. "It sure does when you're in good company."

It was time for her hostess to head out for her weekly appearance at the local Christian church. The American never failed to attend the Sunday service and had tried, more than once, to coerce her friend into attending.

That didn't stop her from trying once more, "Oh, won't you come with me for once? Please—"

"You know, I'm orthodox," Sofiya replied. *And not a very devout one,* she thought, unable to remember the last time *she* had attended a service. "Don't worry; I'll wait for you here." She gave her a mischievous smile. "You know I can't get enough of your terrace."

"Fine, have it your way," Sonia said, standing up. "Timmy's in his office if you need anything."

Sofiya waved her goodbye and leaned back in her chair to bask in the morning sunshine. It wasn't long until Timothy Johnson joined her on the terrace, a glass of whiskey in each hand.

"I thought she would never leave this time," he said, with his youthful smile in full bloom.

"I thought so, too," Sofiya agreed, standing up. She took one glass from his hands and brought it up to her lips. "Let's hope they never find radiation traces in the communion wafers."

"Perish the thought," replied the American.

"Oh, by the way," Sonia said, before taking another sip. "Get ready to stop eating fish."

"Fish?!" His deep brown eyes grew comically wide. "My God, where will that woman's paranoia stop?"

Sofiya chuckled as she finished her drink. Johnson did the same with his, and he placed both glasses on the table the minutes they were empty. An instant later, he had the young woman in his arms; their lips locked. Her fingers lost themselves in his short brown hair, while he pushed the last of his whiskey from his mouth into hers. The Soviet spy swallowed greedily as American Minister-Counsellor Timothy Johnson guided her to his bedroom. His desire showed through the fabric of his soft grey trousers, and she smiled in anticipation as she took off his light-blue shirt. He was already tackling the buttons of her sober dress, revealing an impatient body with exquisite curves.

What was it that Johnson had said that night before taking her on the living room sofa—'bodies speak better than words'? Oh, how right he'd been. And theirs spoke the same language of lust and need.

Naked, Sofiya lay down on her back, spreading her legs in a silent invitation. Johnson accepted the offer, moulding himself along her sinuous curves. Beneath the American's warm hands, Sofiya felt herself coming to life. The man's lips trailed a path on her abdomen, biting and sucking, and she grew more restless with each love bite.

One of Johnson's hands slipped between her legs, and she sighed when he started to rub at her, back and forth. Rising to catch one of her engorged nipples between his teeth, he made a point to caress her everywhere but where she most desired his attention. Sofiya had to fight an impulse to scratch at his back in retaliation. Johnson seemed to perceive her frustration regardless, and he let go of her nipple to duck his head between her tights.

In two months, the two lovers had had ample time to get to know each other's bodies, and each had discovered what drove the other crazy. Johnson's tongue replaced his fingers, and Sofiya moaned without restraint. With both of his hands now free, the American reached for her breasts, squeezing and pulling at intervals.

The young woman clung to his hair, pushing down feverishly so that he would hasten his delicious torture. Johnson dragged it on for a long time, taunting her without ever fully giving in to her demand. He took a perverse pleasure in letting her get close to orgasming, then using pain to bring her back from the brink.

He kept the game going until she was delirious with need. And when he finally licked her where she so desired, Sofiya exploded with a primal scream. Johnson kept sucking and biting on her clitoris as she rode out her orgasm, drenching his chin in her pleasure.

With a victorious smile on his lips, he waited for her to stop trembling to penetrate her. He needed his lover to be present for this—to be focused. She didn't disappoint, bringing their lips together at the end of the first thrust.

Sofiya tasted herself on the American's tongue, and she tightened her legs around him to allow him to get deeper. Johnson groaned in response, his rhythm quickening—their kiss maddening.

Their lips parted when he got too out of breath to continue. And Sofiya could feel that he was close. She arched her back over the sweaty blankets, offering herself more fully to him, and the man's pacing increased. With each one of his strokes, she clenched her pussy a little tighter around his cock. Johnson was too far gone to stop now, moaning Sofiya's name incoherently. For the young Russian, the need to scratch at his back, to mark him somehow, got stronger. She clenched the cotton bedsheets with both hands to stop herself from leaving marks on her partner's body.

Johnson adjusted his position so he could hold himself upright with one hand. Without slowing the rhythm of his thrusts, he grabbed a fistful of her left breast and Sofiya moaned in delight at the mix of pleasure and pain she was so fond of.

She was struck with a second orgasm when he pinched her nipple hard between two fingers. Her pussy clenched his cock tightly, and Johnson wasn't long to join her, exploding deep inside her. He came long and hard and slumped down on her when he was done.

Sofiya wrapped her arms around him as their breathing returned to normal. The American's flaccid cock was still in her, and the smell of sex was thick in the air. She smiled at the thought, enjoying the masculine essence of the man lying on top of her.

He did the same, his face buried in the hollow of her neck. Nothing could disturb this moment of peace and filled emptiness.

Sunday morning was definitely her favourite time of the week.

MONDAY, JUNE 9, 1986.

STOCKHOLM, SWEDEN.

On her way to the Russian Embassy, Sofiya tossed her empty wallet in a bin, along with her purse. Bending down, she grabbed a fistful of dirt and small rubble and pressed it against the side of her face. She rubbed it in, making sure that some of the dirt stayed tucked to her hair. Reaching for a sharp rock, she used it to scratch at her arm, leaving two superficial cuts along her forearm. Then she used it to add strategical cuts to her denim and blouse. When she was done preparing herself, Sofiya looked like she'd been thrown to the ground on a hilltop before she rolled all the way down to the valley below. Reaching a street with a lot of traffic, she hailed a cab, and with tears in her eyes, begged the driver to take her to the Russian Embassy.

Returning home from her meeting with Mikhaïl Serov, Sofiya had spent long hours thinking of an excuse to go to the embassy. Petrov had never invited her to visit his office, and she feared that without a proper excuse, he wouldn't welcome any surprise visits. She had finally settled on faking a mugging, and the subsequent loss of her identity papers.

When the guard minding the Embassy gate told her he couldn't let her in without proper ID, she requested he call Counsellor Petrov, who'd vouch for her.

As she waited for the guard to come back out, she was careful to lean against the side of the security booth as if she were favouring her left foot. She could feel her tears drying up in the caked dirt that hung to her face.

"I'm sorry; the Counsellor isn't in the Embassy at the moment," the guard said, as he came back out.

Sofiya scrunched up her brow, as if deep in thought. "Could you maybe try Minister-Counsellor Alexeïeva, please? I know her, too."

The guard nodded, and he returned inside to place another phone call.

She had no idea where Petrov was, but his absence would only make things easier for her. Her plan was unfolding to perfection. When the guard came back out to tell her that Alexeïeva was going to see her, she feigned a relieved expression.

A plump secretary with thick glasses and greying hair scrunched up in a ponytail soon came to get her. She escorted Sofiya to Madame Minister-Counsellor's office, and Sofiya limped all the way.

"My dear Sofiya," exclaimed Alexeïeva when she first caught sight of her. "What the devil happened to you?"

The young Russian looked up to face the newcomer. "Two men in the park," Sofiya said, panting. "They grabbed my bag."

"Get her glass of water, Natasha," Alexeïeva ordered, "and some tissues." Then she helped Sofiya to her office, indicating that the young woman should sit down in the small leather couch that sat below a window, opposite her desk.

Sofiya obeyed with obvious relief. When Natasha returned with the glass of water, a dried biscuit, and some tissue, the young spy gave her one of her warmest smiles. Anyone who was at the redhead's beck and call deserved a little kindness.

"Oh, you're quite welcome, dear," Natasha said before seeing herself out.

Alexeïeva closed the glass door behind her before shutting off the blinds. Then she came to sit on her desk, perching on its edge like a panther ready to pounce. The kindness with which she had welcomed Sofiya was gone, and a sour fury kindled to life in her eyes.

Sofiya remained silent as she waited for her to open the hostilities. She studied her opponent while she waited. The Minister-Counsellor had untied her hair, and the long, wavy ginger locks cascaded on her shoulders before coming to rest on both sides of her steep v-shaped cleavage. The top of her generous breasts showed above the rim of her black silk blouse. She wore matching high-heeled boots and a pair of very tight-fitting dark-brown corduroy trousers. As always, Alexeïeva was dressed to impress, and the heavily accented makeup she had painted on her face was on par with the rest.

On a woman of her age, that kind of look was borderline vulgar, thought Sofiya, wondering again why Petrov would want to go anywhere near that kind of person.

"How do you like the couch?" asked Alexeïeva. "Comfortable?"

Of all the tools at her disposal, that hadn't been the opening salvo Sofiya expected. She nodded cautiously, "It's —okay."

Alexeïeva smiled a predatory smile. "Yes, Viktor likes it too. We've shared more than one 'comfortable' moment on it." With a chuckle that was more akin to a purr, she added. "Ah, if that leather could talk—"

Sofiya was tempted to laugh in her face. She couldn't care less about how her fiancé spent his free time, and if his standards stooped low enough to include someone at Alexeïeva's level, then so be it.

"Not the kind of story I'm interested in hearing," she said, with an indifferent air.

"Oh, is it not? Then why are you here?"

"As I said," she shrugged her shoulder, wincing when it pulled at one of the cuts on her side, "I was assaulted."

"Oh, yes, so you were. And—" Alexeïeva crossed her arms over her chest, and Sofiya worried that the top buttons of the blouse would pop. "You can cut off the damsel-in-distress act. As you can see, your fiancé isn't here, and I'm not a middle-aged man looking for a cheap fuck."

Always the kind word, thought Sofiya, as she wiped away at what was left of her crocodile tears. Fine, if that was how the redhead wanted to play it.

"That's not why I came looking for Viktor; besides, I think he's already getting all the cheap fucks he needs." *Eat that!* she thought. "A bunch of drunk teens caught me by surprise in the park; they grabbed my bag and threw me in the bushes."

Alexeïeva's jaw tightened at her retort, and scorn coloured her next words, "You could have gone to the police; I believe that's what people do."

"I would have, but my identification papers were in that bag—to my real name." Sofiya sighed. "I'm not sure what the Swedish police would have found had I given it to them, but I thought it best not to risk it."

"You could have gone to them; there's nothing out of the ordinary in your file," said Alexeïeva.

Sofiya let an eyebrow rise at that. *Checking up the competition are you, Svetlana?* she thought with an amused smile.

A soft blush crept up in the redhead's cheeks when she realised what she'd inadvertently revealed. "Well it was a good thing you came to us, then," she hastily said, in a vain attempt to cover up her slip-up. She moved to a nearby cabinet and pulled out a form.

She handed the document to Sofiya along with a pen. "Fill that in. We'll have new papers ready for you by the end of the week."

Sofiya did as was suggested, taking her sweet time to do so. She was halfway through when someone knocked on the door. Alexeïeva went to open it, and Sofiya heard Natasha say, "The Ambassador wants to see you."

A sigh later, the redhead said, "Leave the form on my desk when you're done. Natasha will find someone to drive you home." Sofiya heard no goodbye—only the tip-tapping of the Minister-Counsellor's heels on the cold, hard floor as she walked away.

The young spy dutifully finished filling in the form, then used the tissues and glass of water to clean herself up. The hobo look did its job, but with the redhead gone, she could start to look like herself again. Svetlana Alexeïeva had eyed her like a hawk, from the minute she got in the office, analysing her posture and tone of voice. But Sofiya had been trained to withstand far more difficult interrogation techniques, and she'd played her role to perfection. Had Petrov been present, her goal would have been more difficult to achieve; knowing him, he'd have come up with questions meant to trip her up and destabilise her. But the ginger-haired diplomat, so busy marking her territory like a dog in heat, had been as easy to fool as a child.

Once again, Sofiya wondered at the strange relationship Petrov and Alexeïeva entertained. *If that leather could speak, indeed*, she thought, standing up. She placed the form on the diplomat's desk and returned her pen to the tumbler from which it came. Leaning over the desk as she did so, Sofiya took a long look at the assorted documents on the flat surface. Then, bending down to re-tie her shoelace, she placed the small listening device Serov had given her under Alexeïeva's desk chair.

FRIDAY, JUNE 13, 1986.

STOCKHOLM, SWEDEN.

The SSI had its offices on the outskirts of Stockholm, in Solna. Tucked next to Hoga Park and Brunnsviken Lake stood *Karolinska Universitetssjukhuset,* Sweden's largest university hospital. And next to it, the *Karolinska Institutet,* since 1810, one of the world's leading medical universities. Several pharmaceutical and research companies had their offices on the same street corner, as did the Swedish National Institute of Radiation Protection.

Sofiya wore one of her best disguises to infiltrate the tall glass and concrete office building: that of blandness. She wore a simple pair of dark trousers and an off-white blouse that was a little too large. Her makeup was different, too, and a lot more subtle than usual. She'd applied a matte foundation to hide all kinds of shine and wore no lipstick and various shades of brown eyeshadow to highlight the dark circles beneath her eyes rather than hide them. She'd let her hair loose and brushed it so that the strands had little to no movement to them.

Sofiya knew that beauty attracts attention just as much as

ugliness, but that there is a small area between these two qualities where one can achieve true anonymity. For when physical traits are neither pretty nor ugly, they become —unremarkable.

This anonymity wasn't to be found solely in clothes and makeup; it was in the person's posture, too. Not so slack that it would seem like one was tired or bored; too straight-backed would lean towards pride or rebelliousness. No, a perfect balance had to be found between the two. It was an extremely fine line that Sofiya had to walk if she wanted to blend in with the background to the point of vanishing from awareness.

She came down the street with the gait and facial expression of someone who'd had the same job for many years, and who acted as if on autopilot. A group of three middle-aged women stood by the entrance door, their ID badges at the ready, and Sofiya narrowed the gap with them. Staying half a step behind them assured her onlookers that she was part of their group.

The man minding security flashed their ID badges one by one before letting the four of them in.

The young spy followed the group of women down a corridor. At the end of it, when they turned left to go back to their office, she turned right and headed for the stairs.

On her way to her target, she passed a door labelled "Office Supplies," and she stopped on her tracks. Pushing it open, she stole a pencil and an empty manila folder that she tucked beneath her arm. Then she kept moving forward and mingling with the other employees.

To anyone who glanced up from the documents on their desk, Sofiya looked like a regular employee: glad to have a job but slightly bored of it just the same.

Using Serov's information, she had no trouble finding the office she was looking for. The plaque on the door read, "Regional Director Magnus Sjögren."

Relaxing her shoulders for a moment, she reached a hand up and knocked twice.

"Come in," a voice called through the flimsy panel of wood.

"Morning," she said, pushing the door open. "I need to make copies of," she opened the empty manila folder in her arms and pretended to look for a reference inside, "Report 86–12, please."

The office was medium-sized, with two wooden chairs for visitors and a central oak desk with electrical cords dangling off the edge. On the right stood three rows of shelves filled with binders and manuals. There was a window on the other side.

A man sat behind the desk. In his early sixties, he was busy filling in a report by hand.

Director Sjögren paused in his writing to look up at the newcomer. His weathered face had amiable wrinkles. "What do you need it for?" he asked.

"I have to make three copies," Sofiya said with a shrug of her shoulders. "Don't know what these will be used for, though."

"Are you on Lise's team?" Sjögren asked, standing up.

Though she had no idea who Lise was, the young spy nodded. "It's my first week."

"86–12, was it?" the elderly man asked as he stood to reach the highest shelf.

Sofiya hmmed confirmation and stayed where she was.

"Ah, there we are," Sjögren's fingers fastened on a thick

folder. "The Chernobyl report. Yeah, that's a popular one. Probably someone at the *Riksdag* that wants a copy."

He took it out and handed it to the young woman with a kind smile. "Bring it back when you're done, will you?"

"Sure thing," Sofiya said before taking her leave. She was out of the building ten minutes later with the file in her hand.

Serov was parked in a dark-brown Volvo two streets away from the SSI facility. He saw her coming in the rear-view mirror. The engine whirred to life as she opened the passenger door, and they were off before she had time to fasten her seatbelt.

"Everything went all right?" he asked, taking a turn to join a busier street that headed south and into Stockholm.

"Of course," she said, opening the file she hadn't had time to inspect more closely.

Report 86-12 had been redacted by one Anders Björkman, an analyst, on May 2, 1986. It contained an early chronology of what the Swedes had dubbed the "Chernobyl Emergency".

The report accounted for what happened at Forsmark on the morning of April 28 and detailed the radiation levels recorded. Then came the numbers transmitted by the three other nuclear power plants in Sweden, the ones provided by the Finnish Centre for Radiation and Nuclear Safety, and finally, the contribution from the Risö Research Centre in Denmark.

Sofiya flipped the pages and discovered documents from the FOA, the National Defence Research Institute, and the SMHI, the Swedish Metrological and Hydrological Institute. *Very thorough,* she thought as she kept reading.

Looking at the various timestamps on the documents,

Sofiya had to admit the Swedes had been quick to figure things out. The alarms sounded at Forsmark at 10 am, and the FOA and SMHI reports came in at around 1 pm that same day.

"In less than four hours, they had the numbers to prove that it was a severe nuclear reactor accident and that it had to have come from one of five USSR sites," she said out loud. "What do we need this file for?" she asked.

"We don't," Serov said. "We just need the Swedes not to have it anymore."

"I thought they'd backed off and stopped asking embarrassing questions?" Or had Erik Nilsson not kept his word?

"They have," the man confirmed. "But Moscow would prefer these types of documents to disappear, regardless."

Of course, they did, thought Sofiya; *they wouldn't want historians contradicting their version of the truth.* She knew it was soon to be time for the scholars to update the history books and, as per the Soviet tradition, it was up to the Communist Party to decide what had happened, and no one else.

They kept driving through town, and a thick silence fell on the two Directorate K operatives.

"Anything good come out of the microphone in Svetlana's office?" Sofiya asked to distract herself.

"Her day job is pretty boring," Serov said, a smirk blooming at the corner of his lips. "But what happens when most people leave, and your fiancé drops by, is more interesting—if you're into that kind of stuff."

From the expression on the short man's hawk-like face, Sofiya guessed he *was* into that kind of stuff. "And aside from that?" she asked. "Anything that can be of use to us?"

"Not yet, no—but I would be tempted to trust your

instinct on Svetlana Alexeïeva. I've been tailing her most of the week, and something doesn't add up."

That piqued Sofiya's curiosity. "What do you mean?"

"Her car, the way she dresses, her lifestyle—she shouldn't be able to afford all of that with her salary."

"Have you checked her bank accounts?"

"They're clean, but there aren't that many withdrawals—which is strange, given the wads of cash she keeps handing out to pay for all the Westerners privileges she indulges in."

"She wouldn't be stupid enough to scam off the embassy's accounts," Sofiya spoke her thoughts aloud. "She must have her own sources of income on the side."

"My thinking exactly." Serov took St. Erik's bridge to get onto Kungsholmen island. "And that's what I will focus on."

Once they reached Marieberg, he parked the car two streets away from Sofiya's apartment. "See you on Tuesday," he said as she opened the door to exit. "And congratulations!"

Sofiya froze, the door still in her hand and half-closed.

"I've just learned that your fiancé contacted the civil registry office to ask for a marriage license." Feigning chagrin, Serov added, "I thought we were friends, little bird. And yet, you didn't even tell me the good—"

Sofiya shut the door in his face before turning her back on the car and the man at the wheel. She walked away at a brisk pace, a sour fury coursing through her veins.

Petrov hadn't mentioned the wedding again, and what with the recent events, she thought she'd have more time—guess she was wrong.

SUNDAY, JUNE 22, 1986.

STOCKHOLM, SWEDEN.

The wedding of Sofiya Litvinova and Viktor Petrov was scheduled to take place on Sunday, August 11, 1986, in Moscow. The ceremony would be held in the Cathedral of the Dormition in the Kremlin.

Sofiya had thought that nothing short of a natural catastrophe would stop it from happening. But such an event had occurred, and it did not affect the schedule in the slightest. It would seem that a couple of hundred miles of radioactive wasteland weren't enough to alter Petrov's plans. Even when people all over Europe were advised not to go within 100 kilometres of the Chernobyl site, and that any trip within 500 kilometres of the site should be seriously reconsidered, her fiancé gave no indication of wanting to alter their plans —besides, Moscow was 800 kilometres northeast of Chernobyl, so it really ought to be of no consequence.

Thus, Petrov had chosen which type of dress she should wear and commissioned a tailor, and one of the embassy's secretaries had sent the invitations. Everything had been sorted out in a single day, and Sofiya's input hadn't been needed at all. That night, she drank her fill of vodka to numb the rage.

The nightmare was still real when she woke up the next morning. But the night had allowed her to gain a new perspective. She'd been surprised when Petrov told her where the ceremony was to take place. If asked, she'd have imagined one of Moscow's smallest Russian Orthodox churches, but she'd have been wrong. Not only had her fiancé managed to gain access to a Cathedral, but he'd landed one of the Kremlin's largest.

That was so unlike Petrov. The diplomat thrived on discretion and always made sure to never stand out when in a crowd. Why was he suddenly so determined to make a grand affair out of their farce of a wedding? She knew he had no feelings for her and that their union was only one more part of his stratagem to get the *Komitet* off his back. Why go to such extreme length to sell the lie?

Did this have to do with him being part of the *Nomenklatura*? Was such an extravaganza expected out of someone of his rank? Surely, this couldn't be the only explanation. No—Sofiya was certain her fiancé had an ulterior motive.

The more she thought about it, the more it became obvious to her that this whole thing was a smokescreen meant to hide a darker, more sinister plot, and that everything Petrov had done so far had led him to that point.

That last realisation opened the door to one more question. That night in Moscow, had he decided to let her live because he knew he needed to have a bride on his arm come the summer?

These thoughts followed her as she made her way to Östermalm for her weekly meeting with the Johnsons. She kept trying to figure out Petrov's plans as she listened to Sonia Johnson's advice on marital life. The American woman was so certain that her own marriage was an example of success that she turned into a well of information of spousal dos and don'ts.

Sofiya smiled kindly as she took in her advice with a distracted ear. And she fought not to let her face give away what she would soon be doing in the Johnsons' marital bed, and with whom. When Timothy Johnson removed her lace panties with his teeth only three minutes after his wife had left for church, Sofiya's gruelling thoughts finally quieted.

"Is something bothering you?" the American asked when he'd had enough of the young Soviet staring at the ceiling in silence. Though their little playtime had been passionate and wild, it hadn't been enough to dispel the shadow that hung over Sofiya's face.

"It's nothing," she lied, but in the distance, she could still hear wedding bells ringing.

"It's not nothing; you can confide in me, you know."

If only I could, she thought. Blowing out a deep breath, she straightened and went to look for her discarded clothes.

Johnson pushed himself up on his elbows, "What did I say?"

"Just because we're fucking each other doesn't mean we have to talk to each other!" Sofiya hastened to put on her underwear and green pleated skirt. "I'm going home."

"But what will Sonia say?" asked Johnson as he got out of bed.

"You'll think of some excuse. You lie to her all the time; that's nothing new to you."

The barb had been intended to hurt, and it did. Still naked, the American reached for her. "Oh, that's rich, coming from you." Holding onto one of her wrists, he stopped her from leaving the bedroom.

"Let me go!" Sofiya was fully clothed, and a pair of stilettos dangled from her hand. "You know I can have you down on the ground in no time."

"What's stopping you?" Johnson teased her, with an amused smirk at the corner of his lips.

In one movement, Sofiya dropped the shoes from her hand, while she gripped the man's wrist with the other. Without letting go, she turned on her heel so that she was back to front with him. Using the momentum and years of practice, she flipped him over her shoulder with ease.

Johnson fell flat on his back, in the space between the bed and the wardrobe. As if he'd been expecting it, the American used the woman's grip on his arm to bring her down with him, rolling them both and inverting their position. Sofiya hadn't expected him to know that countermove, and surprise was the only reason he managed to gain the upper hand.

Pinning her down with a knee to her stomach, Johnson reached for her second wrist. He brought them both up above the brunette's head, a wide smile blooming on his lips.

Sofiya tried to wiggle free, but with all of the American's weight atop her, and her hands imprisoned, there was nothing she could do.

"You're my sunshine; you know that?" he said before

leaning down to kiss her. "And in a city like Stockholm, that's no small thing."

Sofiya had no choice but to return the kiss. "If it wasn't for our Sunday mornings, I'd go crazy," she confessed when their lips parted. "Alexeïeva is a hellion, and Petrov is colder than Siberia."

"Let's not talk about your fiancé, please," Johnson begged, with another kiss. "There's something else I want to do."

Sofiya arched an eyebrow at that. "And what if I don't?"

The American chuckled. "I don't think you have much of a choice, Sofiya Litvinova; you're all mine." Tightening his hold on her wrists, he moved up to place both of his knees on either side of her shoulders.

"Now, open up," he commanded, as he lifted his naked hips.

THURSDAY, JUNE 26, 1986.

STOCKHOLM, SWEDEN.

Coming back from her morning run, Sofiya pondered what Serov had just told her. Moscow had approved her union to Viktor Petrov, and the head of Directorate K thought she should try to bear him a child within a year, thus truly cementing their relationship and dispelling any reserves the diplomat might have for her allegiance.

The sick, twisted smile with which Serov had given her the news had made her want to punch him in the face, and quite possibly, in the nether region too. But she'd only tightened her fists as she nodded, like the good soldier she was. She was a child of the nation, after all. She owed everything to the Communist Party; they'd made her who she was, and it was her honour to serve the Soviet Union—or so they thought.

She needed a way out. Petrov had promised her that in Moscow—a way out—if she agreed to help him. Well, it was time his promise became more concrete. Or else she didn't mind facing him with a loaded gun again, even if, this time, he didn't avert his aim.

On the way back to the flat, she pushed herself harder than she normally would. Her legs soon started to burn, and she welcomed the sensation, even as they beat the asphalt harder.

Entering the living room, she removed her trainers and walked straight to the kitchen. She hadn't expected summers in Sweden to be this hot, and she was parched. Pouring herself a glass of water, she took a minute to breathe in and out to recuperate. Her legs would make her pay for that harsh run for a day or two, but the painful sensation was a welcome distraction for her troubled mind.

On her way back to the living room, she froze when she heard a groan of pain. It seemed to have come from the bedroom area, and she immediately turned to head that way. The door to Petrov's room was half-open, and she stopped short of it as she quickly checked her memory. Her fiancé had been long gone by the time she woke up, and she was almost certain his bedroom door had been closed when she left the flat to meet Serov.

She heard a loud exhalation of breath followed by a groan, and she pushed the door open all the way. The bedroom was bathed in light but empty. Entering, she found a shirt by the bathroom door. It was torn and soaked in blood. *The hell*, she thought.

She stepped forward and pulled that door open. Petrov was sitting on the edge of the bathtub with his back to her. Needle in hand, he seemed to be struggling to sew up a large cut on the left side of his torso.

"What happened?" she asked, moving to his side.

He hadn't heard her approach, and his surprise caused his shaking fingers to almost drop the needle.

"Thought you were out," he muttered through clenched teeth.

"I was," Sofiya cleaned her hands at the sink. "And now I'm back."

She dried her hands and kneeled beside him. Her eyes were level with his wound, and she reached out a hand for the needle. Petrov looked down at her with a doubtful expression.

"KGB training," she reminded him. "We learned to suture in year one."

He handed her the needle, and Sofiya took it. Now that she saw the wound from close range, she could tell it came from a knife. *A hunting knife*, she thought, *thick but short blade*. Though the cut was long, Petrov could count himself lucky that it wasn't very deep. His assailant had wounded him on his side, right above the hip bone. There were very few muscle tissues in that area, and the ribcage beneath the skin had probably been what stopped the blade from going deeper and doing any real damage.

Her fiancé had already sutured the lower third of the wound, but he'd made a crude job of it. Leaning closer, she placed a hand on his torso for support, and she felt him shiver. Sofiya ignored it and concentrated on the task at hand, planting the needle in before pulling the black thread through.

Petrov kept his lips sealed while she completed the first stitch. The only signs that he was in pain were the controlled breaths that went in and out of his nose.

"What happened?" she asked, needing to break the silence.

The reply came out through clenched teeth. "Can't you tell?"

Sofiya sighed before plunging the needle in his flesh again. "I meant, who did this?"

"Someone who disagreed with me."

She pulled the thread through and pierced his skin again. "About what?"

"Needed something from him," Petrov said. "We had a difference of opinion on—" he halted to catch a breath "—the price."

"Want me to take a break?" she asked, looking up.

Heavy beads of sweat pearled on the blonde's brow, but he shook his head no.

"Have you taken anything for the pain?" Sofiya asked before resuming her work.

"Couple tabs," he said, in a breath. "Hasn't kicked in yet."

"Keep talking," she advised as she started in on the next stitch. "Focus on something other than the pain." She pulled the thread through, and Petrov's hands came down to grip the rim of the porcelain tub. His knuckles soon turned white.

"What were you buying?" Sofiya asked.

"Nice try," he closed his eyes shut, "little swallow."

The nickname had been meant to put her back in her place, she knew, and in retaliation, she tugged on the thread a little more than was necessary. A small groan escaped the man's throat, and the corner of her mouth curled up in silent victory.

"Fine. Tell me something else then." She finished her stitch. "What about the man who did this to you?"

Petrov reopened his eyes to look down at her, and their gaze met. "I killed him," he said in a monotone. There was no remorse in his face—no sign he'd just admitted to having ended someone's life. If anything, Sofiya thought she caught a glimpse of curiousness in his gaze. It felt as if the man's eyes were searching for something on her face.

Was he trying to gauge her reaction, she wondered; maybe he expected her to be horrified by his confession, to be afraid of him, but she held his gaze without flinching. Death was a common event in their line of work, and she'd seen her fair share of bodies.

She kept holding his gaze, and a hint of surprise reached Petrov's light blue eyes.

"I've got blood on my hands, too," she said, answering the unasked question. *Both literally and figuratively*, she thought, glancing down at the man's blood on her fingers.

The steel behind Petrov's gaze softened for an instant; then, he blinked and looked away. The moment was over, and Sofiya returned her attention to the needle in her hand.

She finished the stitches in silence.

"Bandages?" she asked once she was done.

"Cabinet, over the sink," Petrov said, between two breaths. "Top shelf on the right."

Sofiya stood and cleaned her hands before opening the small cabinet. She found a roll of bandages and tape and brought it back with her.

Petrov was white as a sheet, she noted, and covered in sweat. It made the soft freckles on his skin looked more pronounced than usual. For some reason, he decided to stand up when she reached him, and his legs buckled beneath him. Sofiya had just enough time to catch him and hook a shoulder beneath his good arm.

"Let's get you to bed," she said, as she took most of his weight on the way out of the bathroom. "Between the blood loss and those pills you've taken, you need to lie down."

He let her manhandle him into bed, groaning when the change of position pulled at the fresh stitches.

"Don't lie down right away," she said, placing a hand at his back to stop him from lying down. "I need to bandage your chest, first, to make sure the stitches stay in place."

Petrov leaned on her as he nodded. His eyes fluttered, a sure sign that the adrenaline was starting to run on empty, and his body was giving up the fight.

Sofiya helped him stay upright as she secured the bandage. Though she'd done a good job with the stitches, the man was going to carry a scar for the rest of his life.

It'll be in good company, she thought, glancing at the old bullet wound on his right shoulder. As she fastened the bandage with tape, she noticed another scar she hadn't yet seen on his lower abdomen. Cutting the tape with her teeth, she took a closer look—that one looked surgical.

"Will this be in your next report?" Petrov asked when Sofiya helped him lie down on his back.

Several answers came to mind. She could play dumb and try to tell him that Moscow had backed off, and she'd been without contact for months. Or she could try to lay a trap and promise him her allegiance, come what may.

In the end, she settled for the truth, "Why shouldn't I? That night, you said you'd try to help me get free, but so far, all you've done is use me as they do." She sat up and moved to close the blinds. "I feel like I've exchanged one cage for another."

Once the room was plunged in semi-darkness, she returned to sit on the edge of the bed. Enough light filtered through the blind to allow her to see that the steel was back in Petrov's gaze.

"I haven't forgotten my promise, Sofiya," he said. "I'm working on it; I just need a little more time."

She huffed a laugh. "Then tell me your plan, at least. Hell, maybe I can help." She motioned at his current state, "What good will it do either of us if you get killed, huh?"

He shook his head. "I'm sorry, but I can't. There's too much at stake."

She placed a deliberate hand on his shoulder to still him when it looked as if he was going to sit up. She let her thumb trace circular patterns on his skin in a soothing rhythm. "We don't know each other that well, but I'm not as useless as you think."

"I know. But you are not as free as you think," he sighed, and his eyelids fluttered close. "Moscow has its eye on you and me both, Sofiya. Any misstep from either of us could cost us our lives."

When the motion of her thumb went unnoticed long enough, she allowed the rest of her fingers to pick up the pattern while her thumb moved down to caress his collarbone. Petrov's breathing evened, and he leaned more fully into the mattress and pillows.

Moving closer, Sofiya let the fingers of her right hand graze his stomach, a promise of better things to come. Though the man was wounded, she could think of several ways to help him cope with the pain that didn't need him to lift a muscle.

The fingers of her right hand moved lower, pushing past the waistband of his denim to outline what lay trapped beneath the thick material. Her feather-light touches became more insistent, and she heard Petrov's breath hitch in his throat. She smiled knowing, this time, it had nothing to do with the pain of his injuries. She was about to cup him fully through the denim when cold fingers sneaked up on her. She recoiled in surprise when Petrov pulled her hand away.

"You can stop your little game, Sofiya," he said, without opening his eyes. "I'm not interested."

"I don't know what you mean." She tried pulling her hand out of his grasp, but Petrov held on with surprising strength, given his weakened state.

"You're more deceitful than I am," he said bitterly. "At least I'm honest about my feelings, unlike you."

"Is this what you tell Svetlana Alexeïeva?" Sofiya asked, tugging her arm free. "Is it honesty that drives you between her legs, or are you after something else?"

Petrov's eyes flashed open at that, and he levelled her with a cold, hard stare.

"That's what I thought—you use her just like you use me," she said, with a sour smile. "You can criticise all you want, but you're no better than me."

Despite the pain, Petrov sat up with a wince. "And what of your relationship with Timothy Johnson?" he asked, freezing her on the spot with that piercing gaze of his. "Is that any better?"

A dark laugh escaped his lips at her evident surprise. "Oh, did you think that I wouldn't find out? That I wouldn't know what happens when his wife leaves? Sonia Johnson may be an ignorant fool, but I'm not. Now tell me, little swallow. Is it just the quick release you are after, or are you playing the long game?" His tone darkened. "Is he your backup plan, should I fail to deliver on my promise? Is that it?"

"We're done here," Sofiya said, sitting up.

"No, we're not." Petrov leaned back down. "Since you're so eager to help, I have a mission for you."

FRIDAY, JUNE 27, 1986.

STOCKHOLM, SWEDEN.

Dressed entirely in black, Sofiya left the flat at midnight with Petrov's keys in her hand. She got in the car, turned the ignition on, and the engine roared to life. She was out of the parking lot and heading to the island of Långholmen a minute later.

She took the Västerbron to reach the small island that was just south of Kungsholmen. Once there, she had no trouble finding the right road to reach the remnants of Långholmen Prison. The large building blocks were in the centre of the island. Built between 1874 and 1880, it was once the central prison of Sweden until they'd shut it down in 1975. What was left of it today lay abandoned behind chain-mail fences. There were talks of turning it into a hotel, but for now, it was a popular meeting place of the unsavoury kind.

She parked the car next to some trees and killed the engine. She could see the fence, and the hole in it, from where she was. She reached for the weapon on the passenger seat and placed it in a holster at the small of her back, beneath her black shirt. Then she pulled on a pair of leather gloves and exited the car.

When she'd asked Petrov for more serious tasks, this was not what she'd had in mind.

Cursing at the Scandinavian summer nights and the damn sun that no longer disappeared, Sofiya jogged to the fence and then up to the decrepit building that stood a little further ahead. The dim light gave the tall, off-white building an eerie, ominous look that unsettled her. Though it was the middle of the night, the sky looked as though it was early morning already, and the first rays of the sun had just breached the horizon.

Looking up, Sofiya counted four rows of fourteen windows on this side of the building alone, and that was just one barrack out of at least a dozen. Sparing a thought for the thousands of souls who'd been imprisoned here, she searched for the entrance door.

She found it on the side of the building. With one hand at the small of her back, ready to pull out the weapon, she tried the handle. The door opened, and she entered, silent as a mouse.

There was no light inside, except whatever glow passed through the dirty windows, and she had to pull out a torchlight from her pocket. Having an idea of what she'd find in here, she braced herself before turning it on.

The smell hadn't been enough to prepare her for what lay on the floor just a few feet ahead, and her stomach somersaulted. She recovered quickly and got to work.

From the looks of it, the man Petrov had stabbed in the back hadn't died right away. He'd left a trail of blood behind him as he tried crawling to the front door. He'd breathed his last breath four steps from his goal and two from Sofiya's shoes.

Crouching down, the young woman pulled the blade from the body to inspect it. It was a short army knife and had most likely inflicted the wound that she had stitched up earlier.

"So, he killed you with your own weapon, didn't he?" she said to the corpse before cleaning the weapon on the man's jacket. "Tough luck." Then she pushed it in one of his waistcoat pockets before standing up.

"Well—let's get to it then," she muttered before placing the butt of the flashlight between her teeth. Then she bent down to grab the man's outstretched hands, and she pulled until she reached the door.

Following Petrov's orders, she drove northeast to Östermalm and the docks in the Gärdet district. She easily found her way through the deserted streets and parked the car at the end of a narrow alley between two warehouses.

Leaving her flashlight in the car, she used the bleary midnight sun to open the boot and drag the unknown corpse outside; then, she pulled him to the edge of the pier.

She rolled him on his back and got her first good look at him. He was in his early forties, maybe, with a scruffy beard and hollow cheeks. He had dark hair, and there was a bit of a Mediterranean look to him. Who was he? She wondered. Then she quelled that thought before it led to more questions, like who was waiting for him to come home.

She searched his pockets for his wallet but found none. The only thing her gloved fingers found was a used tissue and several business cards in one of his trousers' back-pockets. Curiosity made her take one out before she pushed the corpse over the edge.

She heard him break the surface an instant later but didn't stick around to find out if he would sink or swim. That man, whoever he was, was ancient history, regardless.

It didn't matter if the police found him in one day or ten. They would never be able to trace him back to the Soviets, anyway.

Returning to the car, she removed her gloves and tossed them on the passenger seat, along with her weapon. She would not need either tonight anymore. Then she reached for the business card in her pockets. "Vittorio Amalfi," she read aloud. "Architect." There was a phone number underneath the name and an address in Södermalm.

This gave Sofiya pause. Though the man seemed to reside in Stockholm, his name was anything but local. Vittorio Amalfi sounded Italian to her ears, and this added to her confusion.

Turning the car around, she headed back to Marieberg as questions arose in her brain. What kind of dealings could Petrov possibility have had with Mr Amalfi? And what was it he'd tried buying from him before their deal turned sour?

SUNDAY, JUNE 29, 1986.

STOCKHOLM, SWEDEN.

After the day she'd just had, anyone who knew Sofiya Litvinova would have expected her to wake up to a pounding headache, a dry mouth, and an empty bottle of vodka on her nightstand. But they'd be wrong.

Sitting up briskly, she stretched and walked to the window. Opening the blinds wide, she heaved in a deep breath as warm rays of lights danced on her skin.

Today, of all days, she was as clear-headed and lucid as an abstinent monk, and twice as determined. Moving to the living room, she placed a phone call to Sonia Johnson to tell her that she wasn't feeling well and wouldn't be able to make it to their weekly brunch. When asked if she thought she would be up for it next week, she remained purposefully vague.

Now that it was clear Petrov knew what she'd been up to, Sofiya doubted she would ever enjoy either of the Americans' company again. Cutting Timothy Johnson out of her life sadly meant cutting his wife out of it, too. With a resigned sigh, she forced herself to think that it was for the better; East and West made for dangerous friendships, after all. But in the privacy of her thoughts, she had to admit that she'd miss their Sunday brunches and the gossiping that came with it. But with the wedding day inching closer and the events of last night still fresh in her mind, she knew she had far more pressing matters to focus on.

For once, Viktor Petrov had shown his true colours, and now, Sofiya knew where she stood with him. Not only had he let her get a glimpse of his true self last night, but he'd also inadvertently given her the description key she badly needed.

Ever since she had met him, she'd been under the impression that Viktor Petrov was playing a role. Day in and day out, that man wore a tight mask that concealed his thoughts as well as his true purpose. Sofiya was certain that everything he said, everything he did, only served to bring him one step closer to his true endgame. Yes, she'd always viewed her fiancé as a chess master executing a careful sequence of moves and countermoves, one scheme at a time.

Ever observant, Sofiya had caught enough tell-tales to make out the outline of his strategy, but the central element that would allow her to unravel the entire structure kept evading her. And thus, she'd remained unable to make sense of the clues she'd gathered.

She chuckled to herself as she sat down on the leather sofa in the living room with a cup of steaming coffee. Who'd have thought the key to unmasking his real persona would be something as tiny and insignificant as a two-inch scar on his lower abdomen. The remnant of an appendectomy; it was the one trace of personal history this secretive man hadn't been able to erase from his life.

Little did Sofiya expect to find it where she had, and at a

time when she wasn't even looking for it. But find it she had, and now the mystery that was Viktor Petrov had started to unravel for her. She held in her hand the master thread in the web of lies the man had woven around himself, and—determined not to let it go—she was going to pull it all the way. For in Russia, she knew, appendectomy scars were never this thin.

Relaxing on the leather sofa, Sofiya allowed a contented smile to grace her lips; she had just found her exit.

TUESDAY, AUGUST 1, 1986.

STOCKHOLM, SWEDEN.

Surprise showed on Sofiya's face when she opened her mailbox. On top of the pile sat a letter addressed to her—the first she'd ever received since moving to Sweden. Inspecting it, she saw that there was no sender, and her name and address had been hastily scribbled in pencil on the front. She tore it open with a fingernail, and her brows furrowed at what she found inside.

The envelope contained a single sheet of white paper, a letter written in the same quick, masculine, blue ink. It wasn't signed, but Sofiya had no trouble guessing at the sender's identity—Timothy Johnson requested a meeting for that very evening.

"Stupid fool," she muttered as she hastened to climb the steps to return to the apartment. Sure, the American had used code-words that she was sure he thought were very clever, but a man like Petrov would have seen through them plain as day.

Sofiya was glad to have come back home before her fiancé did, for she'd have had a hard time explaining the letter's content to him should he have chosen to open her mail—something he probably would have done.

"I missed seeing you during our last communion with the Lord—" it read. "Meet me tonight at the place where I took my first bite of the body of Christ." It was so foolish; it was almost laughable. Retrieving a lighter and an ashtray from a cupboard, Sofiya burned the incriminating letter to ashes.

Looking up at *Storkyrkan*, the cathedral in the centre of Gamla Stan, Sofiya saw that it was nearly seven in the evening. She hurried her steps, mindful of the cobblestones beneath her feet, and reached the hotel right on time. It was the place where Minister-Counsellor Timothy Johnson had taken her nipple between his teeth for the first time and enjoyed "the first bite" he'd mentioned in his letter.

She rode the elevator alone to the top floor with a stiff back, and her hands pushed deep in her coat pockets. She had chosen to dress simply for the encounter. A pair of black jeans and white sneakers with a light-brown raincoat over a simple white t-shirt. She'd also let her hair down and wore little makeup.

Sofiya had no trouble remembering the number of the room the couple had shared for an hour that night. Gathering her thoughts, she tightened the belt of her coat around her waist and inhaled deeply before knocking at the door.

When the American opened, he was shirtless, and he welcomed her with a glass of champagne in his hand.

She declined the offer with a wave of her hand. "I'm not staying," she said, with little warmth.

"What do you mean?" he asked, placing the glass on the

bedside table before coming to stand in front of her. The button of his denim was already undone, and the outline of his penis was starting to show against the fabric.

Sofiya sighed and crossed her arms. She didn't want to have to spell it out for him, but it looked like there'd be no other way. "I only came to tell you that it's over." Johnson's face told her he had a hard time connecting the dots, and she wondered how many glasses of champagne he'd already had. "Us, Timothy," she added. "We're over."

"Is this a new game?" He smiled, drawing closer. "Playing hard to get, are we?" With a chuckle, he pounced on her, encircling her torso with both of his arms.

"Gotcha!" he said, pressing his lips to hers. His tongue sought entrance between her lips, but Sofiya refused it to him. She remained cold and unmoving until realisation dawned on the American that she wasn't playing, and he let go of her.

Sofiya uncrossed her arms and rearranged her coat. "As I said, we're over." She gave him one last emotionless stare before turning on her heel. "Good night."

"What the hell are you playing at, Sofiya?" Johnson reached for her right arm to stop her. With a strong pull, he forced her to turn back. Incomprehension was painted all over his round face. "You can't just say that."

"We are done; get over it!" Working her arm free, she used both hands to push him back. "It was just sex, Tim—an itch that needed to be scratched."

The pain was easy to read in the man's brown eyes. However strange and twisted their relationship had been, he'd made the mistake of letting himself care about her. "You can't mean that, Sofiya. Please, you must come to your senses."

"It's over," she repeated, her tone harder.

"No, you can't mean that. I know you, Sofiya. I know what you need." He was downright begging her now. "We were good together."

Was he pleading for her or himself? Sofiya wondered. With her gone, Timothy Johnson would have no choice but to return to the Stockholm underground scene for faceless birds to fuck in drab hotel rooms. The kind that offered little challenge and whose taste was quickly forgettable.

"You don't know me!" Sofiya all but cried as she forced her cold mask to swallow any sign of sentiment that might show on her face.

"I do know you; I know what you need. What you crave." Johnson took another step closer, his hands outstretched and reaching out for her. "I can give it to you."

Sofiya knew that he could, and therein lay the problem. Despite his inadequacies, the American had managed to bring some colour back to her life. But indulging in her need to fill the void inside her had become too dangerous. It was safer if she went back to her monotonous life of black and white, where she felt like she was half dying and half already dead.

Avoiding his reaching hands, she shoved him back, hard. "Get off me, Counsellor Johnson. We are over; get that through your head."

The use of his formal title and her tone broke something inside the man, and the pleading stopped. Something akin to rage took its place.

"And how will you satisfy it now? That craving?" He asked, with a sneer. "With Petrov? Do you plan on filling that emptiness inside with his fat cock now?"

"Shut—"

He cut her off, his tone rising in volume, "Does he know how much of a depraved slut you are? Does he know what it takes to get you off?"

"You don't know me," Sofiya tried again, but she'd lost some of her countenance.

"Oh, but I do. Bodies speak better than words, remember. You're just like me, Sofiya Litvinova."

"You were a mission!" she shouted in his face. "From the first night in this room, I let you fuck me the way *you* wanted. I gave you what *you* needed, so you would keep me close to you—so I would have access to your apartment, to your private office where you keep official embassy documents." She sneered at him with all the contempt she could muster. "Of course, you thought I liked it, too; that's what I was trained to make you believe. But make no mistake, Minister-Counsellor, I was on orders from Moscow the whole time!"

That seemed to do the trick, and Johnson's rage disappeared as fast as it had come. His face fell, and tears welled up in his eyes as he fought to keep his composure.

"Why are you stopping now, then?" he asked in a small voice, like that of a child begging his mother not to leave him. "When you have what you wanted?"

"Chernobyl changed everything. The Party had to adapt and modify its program as a consequence." With a nasty smile, she said. "Count your blessings and be glad that you have become of no use to us."

"Sofiya—I—"

"Goodbye," she said, turning on her heel for the last time.

This time, the American did nothing to hold her back, and the door closed behind her with loud finality.

The taste of Timothy Johnson still lingered on her mouth when she entered the apartment on Marieberg at eight in the evening. Despite the later hour, the flat was empty, and she wondered at Petrov's absence. Was he busy enjoying some quality time with his mistress while she'd just had to rip out a part of her soul?

She kicked her shoes off before heading barefoot to the liquor cabinet. She cursed when she found the vodka bottle nearly empty. She unscrewed the cap and brought it to her lips.

What little was left in the bottle burned on the way down, and Sofiya thought that maybe it wasn't such a bad thing it was empty. Her endgame was drawing near, and she had better keep a clear head if she didn't want to miss her exit.

Raising the bottle, she toasted the empty room. "To the price of freedom."

FRIDAY, AUGUST 9, 1986.

STOCKHOLM, SWEDEN.

Sometimes the best disguises can be the ones that attract all the attention. And today, a wavy redhead wig, a snug, low-cut leopard-print dress, and overdone makeup that was just the right side of vulgarity was exactly the right combination for the job at hand. Everything about Sofiya was designed to tell a story: the way she'd done her hair, the expensive clothes, and the golden jewellery she wore. People judged books by their covers and individuals by their looks, and Sofiya was dead set on selling the 'rich, middle-aged, comfortable woman' persona tonight.

The cab left her at the entrance to The Strand, a waterfront hotel situated in one of the city's historic buildings. The thick red carpet that took her past the front door cushioned the steps of her tall high-heeled shoes. Sofiya took slow, measured steps, and swayed her hips from side to side as she aimed for the counter. When she reached it, she drummed her fake nails on the marble top until a young girl in an elegant costume, who was barely more than a teenager, turned her way.

"How can I help you, Madam?" she asked, with a practised, polite smile.

"Svetlana Alexeïeva," she said, her Russian accent thick. "I booked a room."

The young woman checked her register and offered her an even larger smile when she found her booking. She handed her a magnetic key card to one of the hotel's finest suites.

"Do you have any bags, Madam?" the young clerk asked, ever so politely. "I can have someone take them upstairs for you if you'd like."

"*Niet*," she said. "One of my men will take care of that later. Are we done here?"

The young woman nodded, and Sofiya left without saying goodbye. Channelling someone as obnoxious and pompous as Minister-Counsellor Alexeïeva was an easy task; she only had to think she was better than everyone else in the room and let her looks do the rest.

Placing the key in her small designer-leather purse, Sofiya headed for the hotel bar rather than her room. Though she was certain the suite was of the finest quality with an astonishing view of Östermalm and Djurgården, she knew she would never set foot in it. She had another mission to accomplish here this evening, and if her intel proved correct, it started at the bar.

She easily found her destination and aimed straight for the counter once she got there. The bar wasn't large. It had about half a dozen dark tables and a long rectangular backlit counter. But with its dim, moody lighting and mirrored walls, the room appeared larger than it actually was.

Sofiya turned quite a few heads on her way to the counter, and she smiled inwardly, even as she pretended not to notice. The crowd in attendance was mostly male, seated in small groups at the various tables with glasses of liquor in one hand and a smoke or a cigar in the other. By the looks of it, they were mostly businessmen. And none of them seemed averse to the idea of spending an hour or two with the ravishing creature that had just crossed the room.

Sofiya paid them no mind, as she ordered a gin and tonic from the young, dark-skinned bartender. She was a little disappointed that there was no music playing in the background to sway her hips to. She'd have expected such a feature in a place like this, but the owners must have thought the thick grey carpeting was enough to smother the ambient sounds.

Using the various mirrors present and the cascading reflections they provided, Sofiya discreetly studied her surroundings and every patron present. Her mark was seated near the back of the room, and he wasn't alone. Two men sat at his table, and judging by their square shoulders, rigid posture, and the familiar bulging shape she could discern beneath their jackets, they were the hired help.

Serov had warned her this wouldn't be an easy mission, but just for once, she could have done with a stroke of luck. By the looks of things, she'd have to play it the hard way once more. The good thing was, she wasn't alone to complete the mission. The bad thing was, she'd have gone with a different kind of help, had she been given a choice.

One table removed from their mark sat a lonely Mikhaïl Serov in a dark-grey business suit, complete with a tie. He was nursing a half-empty glass of vodka on the rocks, looking like a man who needed to relax after a long hard day at the office. He, too, made no effort to hide his interest in the beautiful dame that had just stopped at the counter.

When their gazes met in the mirror's reflection, he gave Sofiya a small smirk before letting his gaze drop to appreciate everything that was put on display.

Sofiya cursed him inwardly but kept her attitude in check. Reaching for the drink that the barman had just placed in front of her, she turned to face the room at large. Placing an elbow on the counter, she pushed her shoulders back and used the twin advantages nature had given her to their full strength. In her head, she started counting to ten. She'd barely reached eight when a middle-aged man, who ought to spend more time at the gym and less drinking beer with his buddies, walked up to her.

"What's a lovely thing like you doing in a place like this all by her lonesome?" he asked in an English that was tinged with an unmistakable American accent. The smell of whiskey was thick on his breath.

Sofiya smiled warmly as she turned to him. "Desperately waiting for some company," she replied in the same language, but with a more eastern accent.

"Well, search no more, baby doll," the man said with a smile that showed he couldn't believe his luck. "You've just found it."

Sofiya chuckled as she took his arm. When it became obvious that he intended to go back to his table, where his two buddies waited with matching incredulous looks, she steered him to the back of the room. "Let's get our own table, shall we?"

Predictably, there was no protest, and Sofiya quickened her step so that she was soon ahead of the man. When she walked past Serov's table, the Directorate K agent emptied his glass before standing up. Acting as if he were leaving the room, he followed the couple as they headed for the last table at the back of the room.

Just as she passed by the mark's table, Sofiya turned on her heel and threw her glass at her date.

"What did you say?" she hollered, loud enough to be heard by everyone and anyone within walking distance. "I don't know who you think I am, but I will not sleep with you for money."

It was hard to tell what surprised the plump businessman more: the gin and tonic that was dripping from his face or the woman's impromptu outburst. Raising both hands up in a placating gesture, he tried stammering an apology, but never got past a mix of 'uh' and 'I'.

Sofiya gave him no time to become more coherent. Stepping back from him, she yelled, "Get your hands off me, you pervert!"

"Everything all right, Miss?" Serov asked as he came to her aid. Without waiting for an answer, he grabbed the poor man from behind. Acting as if he were trying to prevent him from assaulting his victim further, he got a good grasp on the Casanova wannabe.

That seemed to shake the man out of his stupor, and he bellowed, "Le'me go, you prick!" even as he tried fending off Serov. "I haven't done anything."

The Soviet agent may have been a good head shorter than this Casanova, but he was no amateur, and he'd knocked out men twice his size before without breaking a sweat. He gave as good as he got, elbowed the businessman in the guts, and sent him flying to the side.

Casanova landed on the nearest table with a crash and sent drinks and peanuts flying. But Serov wasn't finished with him, and he lunged at him, ready for the second round.

Before he had the time to land the next punch, one of the men that had been seated at that very table stopped him dead in his tracks.

"Let me go," Serov said as he tried getting past the offending arm. "Didn't you see that guy assaulted the lady?"

"I think he's had enough," the taller man said, forcefully pushing Serov back a step. "He's in no shape to hurt anyone anymore tonight."

Serov humphed in displeasure, but he let himself be manhandled backwards, regardless.

"Fine," he said, moving away from the other man's reach. "I was leaving anyway." Straightening his jacket and tie, he gave the poor businessman one last look, which had the man recoil in fear. Then he turned towards the two men that still sat around the table and the one who'd gotten up earlier, and he addressed them with one last parting nod. "Gentlemen."

Sofiya, who'd remained at a good distance from the fight she knew was going to happen, took a few steps closer to the poor man sprawled in a mess of spilled drinks and broken glasses. Looking down at him, she spat, "For the record, there's no amount of money in the world that would convince me to sleep with you."

With that, she turned on her high heel and strutted to the exit, much to the bewilderment of everyone in the room. This was definitely one night everyone here would remember.

Serov was waiting for her in the elevator, using one of his feet to keep the door open. He removed it the instant Sofiya entered the cabin, and the doors closed on them.

"Did you get it?" the young woman asked as she selected the right floor.

Serov smirked at her as he flipped his hand like a magician would, and a magnetic key card slid between his fingers. Subtle, the man may not be, but his reputation as a pickpocket was well-established.

"Get the safe; I'll search the room," Sofiya said, as she entered the room of their mark. "We probably don't have long until they get back."

Serov obeyed, aiming for the only wardrobe in sight. He opened it and crouched in front of the safe as he got to work. Sofiya left him to it and focused on the rest of the room. The microfilm they were after had to be here, but where it had been hidden was anyone's guess. Sure, the safe was the most secure place, but it was also the first spot an enterprising thief would go to.

She opened the night table drawer, lifted the pillows, and passed a hand beneath the mattress. Then she looked beneath the bed and under the lampshades, before deciding that if it wasn't in the safe, it wasn't in this room. She was about to enter the bathroom when the front door lock clicked open—she froze.

With one glance in his direction, she saw that Serov had heard it too. Crouched where he was, on the other side of the bed, there was nothing he could do about it. Dispatching the intruder would be Sofiya's responsibility.

She nodded and pushed the bathroom door open to hide inside. An instant later, the silhouette of a man entered her field of vision. It was one of the guards, and he'd drawn out his pistol. So, they had realized one of their keys was missing, and they expected trouble. Well, she thought, it would be rude of her to disappoint his expectation.

She lunged herself at the man and elbowed him in the side with the full momentum of her action. It sent him flying towards the bed, where Serov was waiting like a tiger trying to catch his prey. The instant the man hit the mattress, Serov pounced on him, going straight for his neck. The security guard tried fending him off, but Serov had a vice-like grip on his windpipe, and he wasn't letting go.

Sofiya forced herself to avert her gaze and return her attention to the front door. She trusted Serov could handle himself against a single opponent, and at the moment, she was more preoccupied with knowing where the second guard was. She didn't have long to wonder, for he'd just entered the room, weapon also drawn.

Sofiya barely had time to move out of the way. A shot rang out, and the bathroom door exploded in a multitude of wood splinters. She kicked off her shoes even as she reached for the toilet seat. She yanked at the wooden lid hard, turned on her heel, and hurled it at her opponent before he had time to fire another shot.

She struck him in the chest and used his momentary surprise to move into a fighting stance and round-kick him in the guts. The toilet lid clattered to the ground at the same time as the man's pistol. The guard would have fallen to the ground under the impact, too, if he wasn't close to the wall. But he was, and backing into it kept him on his feet.

The man was no weakling and, shaking his head to clear his thoughts, he rose both hands up in a boxer's stance. *Just my luck,* thought Sofiya; she'd scored herself a pro fighter.

She mirrored his stance and took a step backwards when the man advanced on her. In this tiny bathroom, she had no way to escape him and little to no weapon at her disposal. The room itself would have to do, she thought, as she feigned a left before throwing the man a right hook. He parried her attack at the last moment and tried a countermove. Sofiya was quicker than him, and she bent down to avoid the punch. Using the momentum, she landed an elbow to the man's gut before retreating to a safe distance again. She wasn't quite fast enough, and the boxer got a grip on her hair. That didn't stop her, though, and the wig was torn free when she swirled on herself to land a punch on the man's face. She heard his nose break; the crunch of bones reverberated over the tiled walls an instant before the man's howl of pain. Speed was Sofiya's ally in this fight, and she wasted no time attacking the guard again. Using the heel of her right foot, she kicked him in the knee, and there was another loud crunch when she hit her target.

Nose gushing blood, face distorted in pain, the man fell to his knees. He tried holding onto the sink for support, but Sofiya knew there would be no getting back up for him. Moving to stand behind him, she grabbed the back of his head with both hands and pushed it into the sink, knocking him out cold.

Bending forward, hands on her hips, she took a minute to get her breathing back under control. When she stood back up, she caught a glimpse of her reflection in the mirror. Her wig cap was askew, and a few rebellious strands had escaped it; sweat pearled at her brow, and her cheeks were flaming red. She looked nothing like the woman who'd entered the bathroom minutes ago.

Side-stepping the unconscious man on the tiled white floor, she retrieved her shoes and wig before returning to the bedroom. Predictably, Serov had won his fight, too. The Soviet agent was seated on the side of the bed, busy rearranging his tie. Behind him, the second guard was sprawled over the coverlet, his neck twisted at an unnatural angle.

"Did you kill him?" Sofiya asked. She hadn't meant for her voice to tremble, but it did, and she clenched her teeth.

Serov barely glanced at her when he stood up. "Why? Didn't you kill yours?"

Sofiya knew better than to reply. Instead, she closed the front door that had remained half-open and then moved to the mirror on the wall next to it. She put the wig back in place and tried to fix her smudged mascara with her fingers. She was lucky the guard hadn't managed to land a blow to her face, for that would have been hard to explain to the wedding guests.

"Found it!" Serov said.

When she glanced his way, Sofiya saw that he was crouched in front of the safe again. So, the mark had gone for the obvious hideout after all. "Good," she said. "We better go before backup arrives."

Serov nodded, and they were out in no time. She didn't know where their mark had gone, but she was in favour of not waiting around to find out. He'd probably moved to another room or had been ordered to wait for backup in a predesignated location. Either way, it was a safe bet that the two gorillas had radioed for help the moment they realised one of their keys was missing.

Sofiya looked like her regular self when she entered the flat on Marieberg. Gone were the wig, the tight-fitting dress, and the over-the-top makeup. She was Sofiya again, a young girl from Moscow who'd made one too many wrong choices in her life. When her eyes settled on the suitcases that waited in the corner of the living room, she wondered if she hadn't just made another one. Same time tomorrow, she would be in Russia, getting ready to marry a man she hardly knew. Her eyes welled up on their own accord, and she had a hard time stopping them from overflowing.

"Sofiya?"

The sound of her name drew her out of her thoughts, and she turned to face Petrov. He'd just come out of the kitchen, and he was looking at her with a curious expression and a touch of concern. She must have looked worse than she thought, she realised.

"I'm fine," she said with a shrug. "Long day."

"I'd ask what you've been up to, but I doubt I'd get a straight answer," he said, leaning against the corridor wall.

"Honesty isn't really part of the job description, is it?"

That got a smirk out of the man. "No, it isn't. Everything is set for this weekend. We can go over the plan one more time if you'd like."

Sofiya shook her head as she walked past him. Right now, all she wanted was a hot shower and some sleep. Her fingers were dirty again, and it wasn't the kind of red stain that could be washed up, even though she knew she'd try anyway.

Why did Serov have to kill that man? she wondered. Murder would no doubt put their covert operation under an official spotlight. There'd be a police investigation, complete with a forensic swipe of the room. Both Soviet operatives had been careful to wipe all their prints, but in their haste to get out, they might have missed something. *And all of that for what?* Sofiya thought, bitterly. She didn't even know what it was they'd stolen, or from whom. Goes to show how much value her own government placed in her. She was nothing but a pawn in their schemes; only good enough to be pushed around to suit their needs—a puppet on Directorate K's strings. It had to stop, or she would go mad.

"Sofiya?" Petrov called out after her retreating form.

"Don't worry," she said, hand on the door handle to her bedroom. "I know what is expected of me; I won't disappoint."

Later that night, as she lay in her bed for what she knew was going to be her last night in Stockholm, she wasn't sure what to feel. She'd enjoyed her time in the Swedish capital and had come to like the meandering town, with all its islands and bridges. She'd come to miss it, she knew. And she could only hope wherever she ended up staying next would be half as nice.

There were so many uncertainties on the horizon that it felt as though her future could be decided with the toss of a coin. And which way it would land was anyone's guess. The only silver lining in her dire situation was the safe bet that she wouldn't go down alone.

Sofiya hadn't chosen a redhead wig for no reason, and she hadn't booked the room in Alexeïeva's name just for fun. For the entirety of the mission, she had made sure none of the cameras ever captured her face. That way, she had ensured that the police would have nothing more to go on than the pixelated image of a bosomy redhead and witness's accounts that she was Russian.

While Sofiya wasn't sure how careful Serov had been in cleaning the bedroom, she knew she'd been thorough with cleaning the bathroom of her prints and strands of synthetic red hair that had been stripped off the wig during the fight. Actually, she was dead certain she left that bathroom spotless —save for the passed-out bodyguard near the sink and the two red hairs she'd dropped behind her on her way out. Two very real human hairs that she'd plucked from Alexeïeva's desk chair when she visited her office.

Yes, it may take the police a day or two to follow that lead to the finish line, but Sofiya was sure they would get to her nemesis eventually. And diplomatic immunity or not, if they decided to dig deeper into that dragon of a woman's life and look at her bank records with a fine-tooth comb, well, it was anyone's guess what they would find.

SUNDAY, AUGUST 11, 1986.

MOSCOW, USSR.

The Dormition Cathedral was the most sacred of the Russian Orthodox churches and stood on the Cathedral Square in the Kremlin of Moscow. Built between 1475 and 1479 by the Italian architect Aristotele Fioravanti di Rodolfo, the building combined Russia's Byzantine heritage with the art and architecture of the Italian Renaissance. With its five tall golden domes covered in gilded copper sheets and its carved limestone exterior, the Cathedral could be seen from miles away.

The interior was as decorated as the richly painted arches of the exteriors, with frescoes as far as the eye could see, on the walls, on the ceilings—the largest one was an image of Christ Pantocrator on the interior of the main dome. Above the altar, the apse was devoted to an image of Mary, Mother of God, standing in a pose that seemed to bless the worshippers.

Sofiya felt small as she walked down the central aisle with a lit candle in her hand. She wore an ivory dress with an embroidered corset and a large gown that touched the ground around her. A thin veil, pinned to the corset around her neck, draped her bare shoulders and fell behind her like a cape. As she locked gazes with the portrait of Mary, Sofiya forced herself not to think of what was really happening within this Cathedral. So much of this *venchanie* was a farce; it was hard not to laugh.

The *svideteli*—the witnesses—were people she had never even met before today. The man, Gregor, was a distant cousin of Petrov, and the woman, Mila, was apparently a friend of his mother, whom he hadn't seen in years. As far as Sofiya could tell, each of them thought this was for real and couldn't believe their luck to be the best man and maid of honour of someone from the *Nomenklatura*—furthermore, at a wedding that took place in the Kremlin.

The betrothal had been a quick affair. Both bride and groom had been blessed by the attending priest at the Cathedral's entrance, and the blessed rings had been placed on their fingers between two prayers. The second part of the ceremony, the crowning, was about to begin, and Sofiya wasn't sure how to feel. A part of her felt like a lamb being led to slaughter, while another couldn't wait to reach out and grab the freedom that was finally in sight.

For Sofiya, the guests in attendance were little more than blurry faces. Aside from her family in the first row, the rest were strangers. For the most part, they were distant contacts of Petrov that had been invited for the form more than out of any real interest. She hadn't been introduced to her soon-to-be mother-in-law, though she knew she was in attendance. "We don't get along," was all the diplomat had said on the matter, and Sofiya had had no choice but to take it in her stride.

In the centre of the church, the couple professed that they

were marrying of their own free will and that they had not promised themselves to another. An *ektenia* and several longer prayers later, the priest placed a crown on the head of the bride and another one on the head of the groom. An *ektenia* and several prayers later, the procession began, and the married couple soon found themselves with the priest's *epitrachelion* tied around their joined hands.

For better or worse, their fate was sealed.

The civil ceremony and tour of the city was a quick affair, and Petrov seemed all too happy when the wedding party returned to the Kremlin for the reception. The guests were, too, if the leering glances towards the buffets and bars were anything to go by.

Sofiya caught up with her parents in the lobby. They had grown apart over the years and, aside from the occasional letter or phone call, she didn't really hear from them much. But that was what happened when your job required you to be abroad for weeks at a time with little to no notice. She discovered that her father had aged even more than she remembered, and his hair, which had once been thick and chestnut brown, was now thinning and silver-white. The years had been a little kinder to her mother, and the wrinkles at the corners of her mouth and eyes gave her an aura of wisdom rather than of old age. Both were dressed in their Sunday best and still looked out of place beneath the ornate crystal chandeliers.

She doubted they'd ever come to the Kremlin before, let alone to its Palace and by invitation. It was no wonder they felt so uncomfortable and didn't know what to do with themselves.

Sofiya wasn't sure what to tell them. Should she lie through her teeth and tell them that she was happy to have finally found the prince of her dreams? Should she prepare them with the fact that this was probably the last time they would see their daughter in this life? In the end, she settled for some warm smiles and platitudes as she escorted them to their table.

When the party began, Sofiya drank champagne for the first toast and moved to vodka for the second. The way it burned on the way down felt grounding, and she itched for another one. But Petrov was already asking for her hand, and a waltz started playing in the background. She had no choice but to give him this dance, but she promised herself it would be the only one tonight.

As they moved and swirled to the cheering and applause of the guests, she tried losing herself in the music. The sea of smiling faces that surrounded them felt suffocating. Aside from her parents and a handful of relatives, all of whom she hadn't seen in over ten years, she barely knew anyone. The only guests she did know were people she wished hadn't been invited: Mikhaïl Serov and Svetlana Alexeïeva.

The first dance ended, and everyone applauded. Sofiya thanked the crowd with a shy smile and a wave of her hand before she moved to the bar to quench her thirst. She planned to drink her way through all the subsequent dancing, singing and gaming. And she'd consider it a bonus if she could wake up tomorrow with no recollection of the day's events.

She was surprised when Serov walked up to her with a reproachful look on his face. She'd expected that kind of behaviour from her husband, or maybe Alexeïeva, but certainly not from her handler. Really, the man ought to be happy with her; she'd done her duty to the best of her abilities and accomplished the impossible. Couldn't he cut her some slack, for once?

"I see your time in the west hasn't improved your manners, little bird?" he said, leaning against the bar.

"I'm not your 'little bird' anymore, Misha," Sofiya replied, unable to keep a soft slur from mangling some of her words. "I'm a married woman now." She pushed her hand in front of his face to illustrate her point. "See!"

He pushed her hand away as if it were offending him. Then, motioning at the empty glass in her hand, he asked, "How many of those have you had?"

"One—no, two." Pouting her lips, Sofiya scrunched up her brow in deep concentration. "Yes, that must be it, two—dozen—give or take."

Her humour was lost on the older man, and he grabbed her wrist when she tried signalling the bartender for a refill.

"Oh, come on, Misha; have one with me." She tried batting her eyes at him, but it had no effect. "It's my wedding, after all; so, let's celebrate."

He pulled at her arm, hard. "You've had enough."

"Let go!" Sofiya ordered.

"Keep your voice down, and don't make a scene." He moved closer, his beady eyes boring holes in hers. His voice was low, but cutting when he said, "Dammit; have you no shame? As an agent of Directorate K, you are expected to conduct yourself better."

Sofiya chuckled but lowered her tone. "And what will you do; put that in your next little report? And then what? I will still be Petrov's wife tomorrow, and the day after that."

Turning towards the barman, she hollered, "Waiter, another one, please?"

The glare Serov sent towards the young man minding the bar led him to quickly reconsider his actions, and he moved to a pile of dirty glasses that needed to be sorted out.

"You've had enough for tonight," Serov said, pulling at Sofiya's wrist as he led her out of the room.

Behind them, the party continued as if nothing had happened. Between the cheering and loud music, Sofiya doubted anyone would notice her absence. Her liaison officer took her down a long corridor and pushed her into a service elevator. With her heels, she had a hard time keeping up with him, but she tried, not wanting to give him the satisfaction of seeing her faltering in her steps. She wasn't *that* drunk yet.

On the second floor, Serov pulled out a key to open one of the numerous doors that lined the corridor, before pushing Sofiya inside. The young woman should have wondered how come he'd had a key to one of the Kremlin's Palace's bedrooms, or better yet, how he'd known there was a free room here in the first place. As it was, she was too tired to care. There was a large bed in the middle of the opulent space, and it looked inviting.

When she let herself fall onto it, the change in stance made her hiccup.

"Now, if you'll excuse me," he said, opening the door. "I need to go and have a word with Svetlana Alexeïeva. Directorate K has certain questions she needs to answer to."

Serov saw himself out, and Sofiya heard the key turn in the lock. She heaved a sigh of relief; her plan was unfolding to perfection—both of her plans, actually. The coast was clear for her, while Alexeïeva's had dark clouds looming on the horizon.

Now that she was alone in the room, Sofiya sat up and wasted no time moving on to the next phase of her plan. She was surprisingly sober, and her nimble fingers started removing layers of her dress. She pulled at the long skirt; it came loose when Velcro parted, revealing a black pair of leggings that were rolled up to the woman's knees. She quickly pulled them all the way down before detaching her corset. She removed the white veil that was pinned to it, flipped the corset inside out, and reattached it. Using some of the spare pins, she brought her hair up before unwrapping the various items that had been strapped to her thighs in lieu of a garter.

There was a small black pouch that she could wear over her shoulder like a backpack, a set of lockpicking tools and a flashlight, and, of course, the map she would need to reach her target.

The last step was unscrewing the heels of her shoes and pulling off the white sheet of plastic that had been taped to the black leather of her slip-on shoes. In no time at all, she had gone from a bride in a white gown to a cat burglar dressed in black.

Less than five minutes later, Sofiya rappelled down the front of the building using the sturdy but fine Kevlar rope that had been hidden in the veil's lining.

MONDAY, AUGUST 12, 1986.

MOSCOW, USSR.

The clock chimed midnight when Sofiya's feet touched the ground outside the Kremlin Grand Palace. She hunched low as she crept along the wall. Thankfully, nights in Moscow were a lot darker than in Stockholm, and the moon wasn't even a quarter full. Sofiya was but a shadow moving through the night.

She reached the Vodovzvodnaya Tower, the corner tower on the southwestern side of the Kremlin, overlooking the Moskva River. She got to the entrance door without being seen and had no trouble picking the lock to enter. Slipping inside, she discovered a lit corridor. Moving as quickly as she dared, she rushed forward, her senses on high alert to detect any officers or guards patrolling.

Following the map that she'd memorised, she turned left at the end of the corridor, and then left again ten feet later, until she reached the staircase she'd been looking for. She climbed down to the lowest level, her rubber-soled shoes making soft whispers on the concrete steps.

There was a crypt in the bowels of the tower, and a chill

ran along Sofiya's spine when she entered it. The cavernous space was entirely made of slabs of dark-grey stone. It was unlit, which added to the eerie feeling emanating from the place. Pulling her small flashlight out of her bag, the young spy flicked it on and continued to move forward.

The light did little to alleviate the creepy feeling in the room, and shadows danced on the floor as they sought to evade the harsh white glow that dared disturb them. Sofiya forced herself to focus on her goal rather than on the various raised tombs and what she knew lay inside.

According to the Italian's map, she was looking for *lo stemma*—the coat of arms. It had been Petrov and Sofiya's hope that the clue would make sense to her once she got here, but it did not.

Too bad we can't ask Vittorio Amalfi what he meant by that, she thought bitterly, remembering the corpse she had surrendered to the depths of Lake Mälaren.

The coat of arms of the Russian Soviet Federative Socialist Republic was composed of wheat, a rising sun, the red star, and of course, the hammer and sickle. This celebration of communism was created in 1918 and, thus, had no place in an old basement like this one.

Sofiya closed her eyes to better remember what came before. Was it the Russian Empire and its great circular coat of arms? In the centre, black on yellow, was the traditional two-headed eagle. It was flanked by the archangels Michael and Gabriel, themselves encircled by the 15 coats of arms of the Empire's territories.

The crowned, two-headed eagle, a powerful mythical creature, had been the symbol of Russia ever since Ivan the Great and the end of the Byzantine Empire. Dozens of variations of the emblem had been made throughout the centuries, but always, the eagle remained. And for several hundreds of years now, it held, in its left paw, a golden sceptre, and in its right, a *globus cruciger*; the symbols of the ruling power and the church—power and dominion over all men.

Looking around at the small room she was in, Sofiya found none of that. Everything here was old, covered in dust, and unadorned. The walls were barren of emblems and symbols and only carried a couple of dried-up oil lamps. The rectangular room had no furniture—no painting or sculpture of any kind. There was nothing here, aside from the eight tombs she had spotted earlier.

Despite her uneasiness, she moved closer to the first one. As raised tombs went, this was a simple one. Four slabs of dark grey stone, one for each side, and a fifth rectangular one to serve as a lid. Sofiya blew a breath over the top surface, and a cloud of dust lifted to reveal parts of the name of the man buried here. She had to use a hand to wipe the surface to read it in its entirety. *Fyodor Godunov, died 15 March 1604.*

Sofiya moved to the next tomb and repeated the action, only to discover that Mikhail Mikhailovich had died on the same date. She continued, discovering the names of these men until she reached tomb number five. This one had no name on its surface, only a carved symbol: a two-headed eagle.

She inspected the tomb more closely but could find no mechanism or button to press. Aside from the emblem on the lid, it looked like the other ones. "Please, be empty," she murmured as she pushed the lid with both hands.

Drawing in a deep breath, she had to put all her weight into the motion for it to begin to slide over. The first inch was the hardest, and she kept pushing until she managed to get it three-quarters of the way off. Bracing herself, Sofiya used her light to reveal the interior. She let out a relieved sigh when she didn't find a decayed, centuries-old skeleton. Instead, she found a steep staircase with steps made of the same dark-grey stone as the tombs.

Flashlight in hand, Sofiya slid herself inside the tomb. Some thirty steps later, she reached the beginning of a dark corridor. It was a well-known fact that each medieval fortress had secret passages and tunnels underneath it, and the Kremlin was no exception. Many of these were believed to have been built in the time of Prince Dmitry Donskoy, who ruled Moscow for 30 years, beginning in 1359. Under his order, underground pathways were built beneath the Kremlin fortress as a secret passageway to the outside. They were to be used by government spies, as an escape route if the Kremlin were besieged and to bring water in from the river during times of war. The fortifications of both the original wooden Kremlin and of the white-stone fortress, built under Donskoy, did not survive the centuries, and a large remodelling was made in the late 15th century by Ivan the Great. It was he who decided to invite renowned Italian architects to build the brick walls and towers, the churches, and the palace of the Grand Duke. The Italians also created the Kremlin's basic underground structures that remain to this day—it was, after all, a must-have for any fortress at the time.

Though few historical documents refer to tunnels, and Soviet officials never mentioned them, the Italians kept some of the original plans in their archives. And that was what Vittorio Amalfi had sold to Petrov for the price of his own life. How that greedy architect had come by them in the first place, Sofiya had no idea, but she hoped the blueprint she pulled out of her backpack was accurate, lest she'd be wandering the meandering corridors until the end of time.

Balancing the flashlight and the map in her hand, she slowly headed north. Her destination, the Arsenal, was at the opposite end of the Kremlin, and she'd have to cross through the entire square to get there. On the surface, that would have taken her less than ten minutes, but down here, she was forced to follow one tunnel after another, and she had no idea how long that would take her. Providing none of the paths she'd selected were obstructed, she estimated it would take her around fifteen minutes, but if she had to re-route on the way—there was no telling how long she would have to trudge through the citadel's belly.

Her target, the former armoury, remained in use as the home to the Kremlin Regiment, the main security service for the Soviet President. On the surface, it was a large elongated trapezoid two-storey building, with yellow-painted brick walls. But below the surface, it was another matter, as Sofiya had recently found out. There was a maze of vaults and chambers, all connected by sinuous tunnels that people had forgotten about.

Keeping a steady pace, Sofiya advanced in the darkness. Aside from the glow of her light, the tunnels were pitch black and smelled of must and mould. The dust had settled on the slab floors, and spiderwebs dangled from crack to crack in the brick walls. The gullet was just wide enough for one person to fit through and barely high enough for her to stand to her full height, and every now and then, she had to duck to pass beneath a wooden beam.

Sofiya checked her map at every junction, pushing forward through dust and decay. The further she went, the thicker the stale smell grew. Fresh air became a rare commodity in the Kremlin's bowels, and she felt herself grow faint. She was forced to slow down to regulate her oxygen intake.

At the turn of a corridor, the path widened, and Sofiya's hopes of finding the exit surged. They were crushed when she stumbled upon a wide chamber and three skeletons lying on the floor. The prisoners still had sturdy iron shackles on their wrists and ankles, and the remnants of moth-eaten clothes on their backs. It looked as if they'd been forgotten down here, for God knows how many hundreds of years. Sparing a thought for the poor souls, she pushed forward. There was another corridor on the other side, and Sofiya headed that way.

Knowing now what fate would befall her should she get caught, she slowed her pace even more to not make a sound at all. The corridor turned left and started to incline upwards. Glancing down at the map, Sofiya knew she had to be close to the exit now.

When the ground beneath her feet started to shake, and dust fell off the stone walls, the air became even more difficult to breathe. The young woman froze as a low rumble grew nearer, reverberating off the walls and echoing down the entire length of the corridor. Sofiya flicked her flashlight off as she waited, motionless. The burbling noise built up, louder and louder before it faded to nothingness again.

"Metro–2," muttered Sofiya in a reedy whisper. It was the only thing that made sense. Flicking the flashlight back on, she got going again. More than an urban legend, Metro–2 was believed to have been built simultaneously with the Moscow Metro to ensure emergency transport links between the most important defence and government facilities and to evacuate the staff of senior state structures in the event of an attack. The secret lines ran deep beneath the city and, she guessed, right below this very tunnel.

When the incline beneath her feet steepened, and the air became more breathable, Sofiya's anticipation of finding the way out intensified. Her long trek through the past was rewarded when, at the next turn, a large wooden door was revealed. She tried pushing it open, but the thick iron hinges refused to move.

Peering at it more closely, she noticed there was a key in the lock; it was made of iron, too, and looked old and rusty. Praying that the room on the other side was empty, she turned it as slowly and softly as she could, only to realise the key wasn't the only part that was old and rusty. The entire mechanism was gritted, and she struggled to move the key. It finally turned, and the latch opened with a loud *clang*.

Sofiya held her breath—if someone was on the other side, there was no way they didn't hear her. She let a full minute pass by before she dared to open the door.

She was surprised to find herself in a cellar. On both sides, and as far as the eye could see, were tall shelves stacked to the brim with a variety of dust-covered wine bottles. She moved closer to inspect the labels and found French red wines dating as far back as the 17th Century.

"And they call this an Armoury," she tsked.

She was tempted to open one at random for a sip or two. The journey through the tunnels, with its dry, stale air and age-old dust, had left her parched. She fought the instinct; the mission wasn't over, and she needed to keep her wits about her. On the way back, though…

Folding the map, she placed it back in her pocket. Crossing through the cellar, she found a staircase that led into the north wing of the Armoury. She climbed up as silently as she could and used Petrov's intel to navigate the building until she reached her target.

The next door she found in her path wasn't as easy to crack as the last one had been. This one had a biometric lock, and there was no tool in her leather pouch that would allow her to circumvent such an advanced system. She reached for a little zipped bag that she had in her bag and, with careful movements, pulled out a small piece of silicone.

"This had better work," she muttered to herself as she turned it face down before pressing it to the sensor with her thumb.

A little green light moved up and down as it scanned what the machine perceived to be a human finger. When the machine bipped, and a red light appeared, Sofiya cursed beneath her breath.

She lifted the piece of silicone, counted to ten in her head, and applied it to the surface again, this time adding a little more pressure. The scanner activated again, moving up and down, and the wait seemed infinite. A bip later, the door unlocked, and Sofiya let out the breath she'd been holding in with relief. She pocketed the fake fingerprint and entered the Armoury's secured vault number 3.

She had General Igorov to thank for granting her access to the Ministry of Defence's private vault. Not that he would ever know he had—but what else did the man expect, leaving his vodka glass behind after leaving the Marieberg flat? Actually, a small part of her hoped that officers with a higher rank than Igorov would one day figure out that it was him that the enemy had used to get to the file; then, there truly would be karma justice to this world.

The room wasn't as large as she'd imagined, but then again, this was one vault out of the six hidden at the

Armoury, so there was still plenty of space for the Motherland to hide its dirty laundry. Barely three-by-four metres, the room was stacked with shelves from floor to ceiling on both sides. All of them were full of cardboard archive boxes with handwritten labels. According to Petrov's intel, she needed the one that said 'Pegasus' on the front. It was the codename for the list of all the Soviet spies undercover outside of the USSR at the present time. The list was updated once a week and existed in only two exemplars: one that was encoded on a medallion that the KGB director kept on him at all times, and another that was hidden here, in a place where no one would ever think to look—well, almost no one.

Viktor Petrov was waiting for her return in the bedroom when Sofiya climbed back in through the window. Serov must have given him the key, she thought. It probably came with a scathing comment about her behaviour during the reception.

The young spy smiled to herself; the irony of the situation hadn't escaped her. For all intents and purposes, Mikhaïl Serov was her alibi for the night. The Directorate K officer had escorted her to a bedroom on the second floor and locked her inside himself. Should there ever be an inquiry as to the guests' whereabouts tonight, Sofiya would be cleared without second thoughts, thanks to him.

Though he'd removed his custom-tailored black jacket, Petrov still wore the rest of his wedding suit. Beneath the perfectly groomed exterior, he looked tired and worried.

"How did it go?" he asked, unable to hide his eagerness to know the answer. Whether he worried for his wife's safety or the completion of the mission, Sofiya wasn't sure—knowing the man, she figured it was for the latter.

"Fine," she said, patting the backpack that she now balanced on one shoulder. "I took pictures of everything."

She closed the window behind her and turned to see something she had never seen before. Petrov smiled. It was not one of his faked, politician smiles, but rather, an honest gesture that betrayed happiness, relief, and pride—all at once.

"It's over?" he said, in a breath. "It's truly over."

He moved backwards until the back of his legs hit the bed, and he let himself fall on the soft mattress. The wave of relief that hit him was so intense, it looked as if all energy had been drained out of him.

Sofiya remained by the window, unsure of what to do. This was a new side of Petrov, human and without a mask. She wasn't used to it, and it left her unsettled. As she looked around, she noticed that both their suitcases had been brought to the room. She hoped he'd been the one to take them there, rather than a bellboy who may have noticed her absence. She was tempted to ask him about it, then thought better of it. It was Viktor Petrov, after all: the man with plans within plans. His name and such a stupid mistake didn't belong in the same sentence.

She moved to her suitcase and knelt down to open it. Moving her stuff to one side, she pulled at the lining at the back until the Velcro strap released its hold. She placed the small backpack there, along with every precious thing it contained. Then she fastened the lining back in place and spread the clothes in front of it evenly.

She was tired and could do with a shower. But this bedroom only had one door, and it led to the corridor, not an in-suite bathroom. Thinking Plan B would have to do, she untied her hair and removed the black leggings and corset that reeked of the stale smell she had picked up in the tunnels. She'd been up for nearly twenty-four hours, and she looked at the bed longingly. As she glanced at it, she found two light-blue orbs following her every move.

For the first time, Viktor Petrov was looking at her with growing interest. While in Stockholm, Sofiya had tried more than once to arouse him. She'd used all the tools of the trade on her target, such as high-end fabrics and suggestive perfumes, but never once had he spared her an interested glance. Tonight, though, it seemed the young woman in a pair of simple black cotton bra and panties, with her messy hair undone, had caught his interest. Sofiya was tired, covered in grime and dust, and had never felt less sexy and appealing in her life, but Petrov seemed enraptured. He reached out a hand to her, and she moved forward to take it. Sofiya expected it to be cold, but it was the opposite. She held on to him, and he tugged until she was right in front of him.

"Thank you," he murmured. "For helping me."

She nodded, stepping closer until their knees touched. When he made no move to escape their proximity, she parted her legs to sit astride his. Petrov tensed with anticipation, and she straddled him fully. Their eyes met, and each one held the other's gaze.

When the diplomat brought both of his hands up to encircle the young woman's shoulders, Sofiya quivered beneath his warm touch. In response, she thrust her hips forward—an open invitation for more. Petrov responded in kind, his hands sliding down to unclasp her bra.

It fell to the floor without a sound, and she expected him

to look down to discover what its absence revealed. The man's icy-blue gaze never wavered from her face, and she moved forward to kiss him. Their mouths found each other, and so began a slow celebratory ballet.

Perhaps it was residual adrenaline coursing through her veins, perhaps it was the freedom she knew was within her grasp, but as she captured Petrov's lips in hers, Sofiya felt more alive than ever. The man's lips parted underneath hers, and she was afforded her first taste of that elusive man she'd pursued for so long. It was nothing like what she'd imagined, for never had she thought that he could feel so warm, so human.

In the distance, Sofiya could still hear the echoes of music and their guests partying and dancing below. But in the privacy of what was to be their nuptial room, their lips and tongues did a dance of their own. Clothes fell to the floor in messy lumps as bedsheets were pushed aside, and passion surged.

In a display of grace and agility, Sofiya settled herself in the middle of the large bed, naked and inviting. She lay on her back, with her head and shoulders resting on the fluffy pillows. The position made her breasts thrust upwards, an indication that she was ready and eager for more. Petrov showed all the signs of being in a similar state, but still, he took an instant to admire his partner before moving forward. His gaze was like a caress on her skin and, when he joined her on the bed, his hands replaced his eyes.

Their movements were neither rushed nor forceful. Each took their time exploring the other, leaving trails of caresses and kisses along the way. Their hands stroked and cupped at everything they could reach, never seeming to have enough.

Sofiya was the first to orgasm, under Petrov's gentle and

deft fingers. Without rushing it, he'd let his partner's pleasure build up until she climaxed. And when the pleasure weave overtook her, he pressed his lips to hers, sipping up all her cries and moans as she rode it out. As soon as she was recovered, Sofiya returned the favour until it was time for her mouth to swallow the evidence of the man's ecstasy.

Outside, light-pink hues tinged the night sky as the first tell-tales of the morning appeared, but neither Sofiya nor Petrov noticed them. Nothing mattered to the couple, but the small space in which they existed as one. They held onto each other with all the strength they had as Petrov moved in and out of her, sharing the common fear that the other would disappear if either one let go. Covered in sweat, aching for that sweet release, they came one more time with their lips sealed together.

In that instant, they had thoughts for nothing more than the moment they shared: a memory that existed outside of time and that belonged to them only. There would be ample opportunity, later, to consider their actions of the night and the repercussions they were sure to have on the European continent and history at large. But for now, passion devoured them alive, and that was enough.

Later that day, Mr and Mrs Petrov enjoyed their first afternoon as husband and wife by taking a walk in the summer breeze that fluttered through Moscow. Hand-in-hand like all newlyweds, they walked around the red square and then followed the Moskova River until they reached Gorki Park. Near the pond, they stopped at a restaurant and had a late lunch on its terrace.

Sofiya pondered what her life would be like now as she dug into her bowl of *Shchi*. The chef had added sauerkraut and pickle to the cabbage and potato soup, and it was particularly sour and just how she liked it best.

This would probably be her last *Shchi* for a long time, she realised, and the good moment she was enjoying turned bittersweet. Like many things, the ingredients to make *Shchi* could be found anywhere, but she knew the result would always taste better in the land of her birth.

Shchi wouldn't be the only thing she'd soon come to miss, she knew, but she'd made her choice, and there was no way back now. It was her belief that the tapestry of a person's life was woven with a single thread. How its colour changed was defined by the multitude of choices a person made every day. Left or right, sugar or salt—and the tapestry grew to paint a straightforward picture. The motive was easy to guess at, except when large forks occurred, and the design was irrevocably altered as a result.

She knew the day her parents agreed to let her join the ranks of the FCD stood out in her design. That ill-fated decision had shaped everything that followed, a crimson stain that bled into every aspect of her life from that point forward. She had been fifteen when it happened, and it took nineteen years and one more life-altering choice for the pattern to change again.

On their way out of the park, Sofiya stifled a yawn. The night had been short, and as fatigue crept in, the newlyweds chose to take a cab back to their hotel.

Petrov hailed a beat-up maize yellow Lada, and they sat at the back. Glad to be seated, Sofiya lost herself in the passing by scenery as they followed the Moskova River once more.

When she felt the car slow down, she looked up and saw

that the Kremlin was still half a mile away. Directing her gaze ahead, she saw that they were coming upon an intersection, and the light had just turned red. Crawling its way to the white line, the driver slowed and only returned pressure to the gas pedal when the light turned green.

They'd almost reached the middle of the intersection when something caught Sofiya's attention, and she turned to the left to look out of the window. She felt her eyes widen and her mouth open in surprise at what she discovered. A scream built up in her throat, clawing its way up her oesophagus, but it never got a chance to make it past her lips—the lorry hit them first.

The world tilted sideways, and both left-side windows exploded in a shower of cutting shards while the metallic body of the old Lada yawned in protest. The car tilted over, and Sofiya was jerked to the side. Suddenly Petrov was there, pressed against her, or rather, she was pressed into him. Pure reflex had her clinging to his arm as hard as she could. Behind the man's strong shoulder, she saw black asphalt rush by, beneath a broken window that was mangled beyond recognition.

Pain registered an instant later; it exploded within her, much like the window had. Nerve endings fired up as one, everywhere and nowhere at once, and Sofiya couldn't make sense of the notion. She tried screaming again, but the darkness that swallowed her stole her breath first.

THURSDAY, SEPTEMBER 3, 1986.

In Moscow, an official report bearing the KGB seal on the front page was secured in the *Komitet*'s archives on the morning of September 3, 1986. It contained the official inquiry report on the death of Soviet diplomat Viktor Petrov and his wife, Directorate K agent Sofiya Petrova (née Litvinova). Their deaths were logged as road accidents and recorded to have happened on August 12, 1986, at 4:30 pm, in Moscow.

A summary of the investigation's findings reported that though the first respondents got to the scene quickly, nothing could be done for the diplomat and his wife. The two of them, along with cab driver Piotr Rachmaninoff, perished in the flames that engulfed the vehicle instants after the collision. Prison parolee and lorry driver, Nikolaï Anatoliev, also died on the scene. Though further analyses revealed a high level of alcohol in the driver's blood, Anatoliev's cause of death was logged as resulting from a broken neck sustained during the initial impact.

The last paragraph of the report detailed that the families

of the deceased were notified the day after the accident by city officials and that the victims' bodies were returned to their loved ones after the investigation was closed to the satisfaction of the KGB.

Near the end of the morning, in London—some seventeen hundred miles away, on the south bank of the Thames River—a different report bearing the MI6 crest was approved.

Mission director, Ian Kenneth, placed report 783AB8 in a manila folder, with a satisfied pat of his hand. This mission had been one of the agency's most ambitious to date, and one of Kenneth's proudest achievements. With a total length of almost nine years, it was also one of the longest to date. Kenneth gave the report one last proud, and almost affectionate look, before handing it to his assistant, Joanne. The young woman sealed it and applied a thick, red 'Confidential' stamp on its front. A couple of hours later, the main archivist, Kenny Stubbs, took it to sub-level three, and placed it in an archive box with the other successful missions concluded in August 1986.

London's report read, "Mission Red Lies was completed on August 11, 1986, when our agent successfully acquired the list of all undercover Soviet spies currently in activity throughout the globe. The next day, agent Andrews and his asset were extracted by our services under the cover of a car crash. The bodies of recently deceased Muscovites were placed in the car rubble in their stead. The car was then set on fire to compromise evidence and render any definite identification of the bodies impossible. The complete report of agent Andrew's infiltration of the Soviet Union under the alias Viktor Petrov, and subsequent nomination as Counsellor to the Russian Embassy in Stockholm, can be found in file 2568-25B.

Agent Andrews is hereby returned to civilian life with a special commendation. For his own protection, he is awarded the new identity #19860228. His asset, Sofiya Petrova-Litvinova, is granted political asylum within our country for service rendered to the nation; she is awarded the new identity #19860229."

Early that afternoon—some three hundred miles west of Vauxhall, in the small Cornish village of Sennen—the inhabitants of Cove Road got their first look at their new neighbours. To the residents' surprise, the young couple unloaded uncharacteristically few boxes from their gleaming, top-of-the-range dark-blue Volvo car.

Less than an hour after their arrival, they pushed open their garden gate to head out for a walk, hand-in-hand.

The man was tall with short blonde hair that was just the right length to curl at the extremities and the beginning of a scruffy beard. On his face stood high cheekbones, an aquiline nose, and a pair of bright and luminous eyes that carried a sunshine-though-misty-foggy-air feel to them. On his lips, he wore a smile that transformed him from someone menacing into someone you wished you knew.

The woman by his side, with her pixie haircut, was almost as tall as he was and graceful in her every move. Though she wore simple clothes, faded denim, and a loose cotton white shirt, she had a poise and allure to her reminiscent of that of a former ballet dancer. Wide green eyes illuminated her delicate oval face, and on her lips hung a charmingly innocent smile that was infectious.

Laura and James Stanton walked hand-in-hand until they reached the coast and the high cliffs that overlooked the Atlantic Ocean. The day was warm, and the sea breeze accompanied them as they headed south on the old southwest coast path. Curling around rugged granite cliffs, the old footpath took them to Land's End, the extreme westerly point of England.

Amazed at the sight, Sofiya gazed at the open sea at her feet, and her eyes lost themselves in that vast ocean of blue. It stretched to the west as far as the eye could see, and further still. For the first time in her life, she felt capable of forgetting the country that lay so far away at her back. Inhaling the salty sea breeze, she realised she was ready to start a new life: one without masks and lies.

By her side, the man formerly known as Viktor Petrov held her hand tighter in his, a silent promise that he wanted the same thing.

"Thank you," she said, turning to face him. "For keeping your promise."

"You're very welcome, my love," he said, bringing her hand up to lay a chaste kiss on her porcelain white knuckles. The golden band of her wedding ring caught a stray ray of sunshine and reflected it in the man's light blue eyes. He leaned forward and pressed his lips to hers, and this was another moment that belonged to no one else but them. This kiss was like their relationship—soft and chaste, respectful and undemanding—and Sofiya smiled into it.

At the couple's back, two thousand miles east of Cornwall, the Soviet Union was standing on its last leg. As Sofiya had feared, the fallout of the Chernobyl disaster was the last straw that broke the camel's back of a frail economy already undermined by an endless war in Afghanistan.

In the not-too-distant future, the subsequently attempted reforms will leave the Soviet Union unwilling to rebuff challenges to its control in Eastern Europe. During 1989 and 1990, the Berlin Wall will come down, borders will open, and free elections will oust communist regimes everywhere in Eastern Europe.

Finally, in late 1991, the Soviet Union itself will dissolve into its component republics, and the Iron Curtain will be lifted once and for all as the Cold War comes to an end.

THE END

NOTE FROM THE AUTHOR

THANKS FOR READING!

If you loved this book and have a moment to spare, I would really appreciate a short review where you bought it. Your help in spreading the word is gratefully appreciated.

FURTHER READING

THE NEVE & EGAN CASES SERIES

A BOLD STUDENT. A SIGHTLESS PROFESSOR. AND A PRIVATE EYE BUSINESS THAT GROWS DEADLIER BY THE DAY...

University student turned PI Alexandra Neve leaves no stone unturned. And when her keen instincts combine with her blind partner's analytical mind, the crime-solving pair sniffs out clues others can't see. But with mafia conspiracies to crack, looted WWII treasure to recover, and captive ballerinas to rescue, the duo can barely keep up with their never-ending caseload.

As Neve and Egan's sleuthing abilities grow with each case, dangerous new crimes take them to the brink of destruction. And with the London streets hiding deadly mobs and madmen, the unlikely pair must keep on their toes... before they end up underground.

Will the two rookie PIs survive to full-fledged pros before their new calling turns deadly?

FURTHER READING

The Neve & Egan Cases Box Set contains four rollicking full-length mysteries. If you like courageous characters, puzzling plots, and non-stop clue-cracking, then you'll love Cristelle Comby's captivating adventures.

FURTHER READING

VALE INVESTIGATION SERIES

MEET BELLAMY VALE, A WORN-OUT GUMSHOE TRYING TO AVERT THE APOCALYPSE, ONE FIGHT AT A TIME...

PI Bellamy Vale's immortality is exhausting. Solving endless supernatural crimes may keep the bill collectors at bay, but the deal he made with a demon is taking a heavy toll on his mind.

Fighting back monsters from the underworld, booting out paranormal predators, and dodging dubious deities, Vale fears being able to interrogate the recently deceased wasn't worth the price of his soul. And as he doggedly attempts to do the devil's dirty work, the scrappy detective could find his ill-gotten powers aren't enough to save him from oblivion.

Can he dispatch the worst fiends of the darkness without triggering a universe-shattering nightmare?

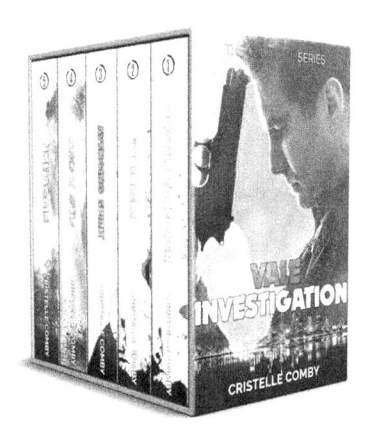

Vale Investigation - Box Set contains the wickedly rollicking five books in the Vale Investigation urban fantasy series. If you like sarcastic private eyes, magical mayhem, and noir-style humor, then you'll love Cristelle Comby's otherworldly collection.

FURTHER READING

ALONE TOGETHER

THEY NEED ALL THEIR WITS TO SURVIVE. BUT A LANGUAGE BARRIER COULD LEAVE THEM DEAD IN THE WATER.

Anne-Marie Legrand is excited to begin her career as an au pair in Sweden. But when the young Swiss woman's flight from Geneva is struck by lightning, both the plane and her dreams come crashing down to Earth. Waking up bloodied and confused, she's terrified when she discovers the only other survivor is a middle-aged man muttering in a foreign tongue.

Scottish banker Killian Gordon may be a world traveler, but he knows next to nothing about wilderness survival. Stuck with a woman he can't understand, he struggles to take charge of the mismatched pair as they explore their surroundings. But the untamed land and endless sea surrounding them tells him no one will be coming to their rescue.

Focusing her efforts on building a sturdy shelter, Anne-

FURTHER READING

Marie battles to keep morale alive with her disgruntled comrade. But with days on the island turning into weeks, Killian fears the odds of living through this nightmare are rapidly declining as the looming Scandinavian winter ensures a lonely and frozen death.

Will they face an even crueler fate than their fellow passengers?

Alone Together is a standalone survival novel. If you enjoy unlikely duos, dramatic landscapes, and adrenaline-fueled endurance, then you'll love Cristelle Comby's desperate tale of stamina and strength.

ABOUT THE AUTHOR

Cristelle Comby was born and raised in the French-speaking area of Switzerland, on the shores of Lake Geneva, where she still resides.

She attributes to her origins her ever-peaceful nature and her undying love for chocolate. She has a passion for art, which also includes an interest in drawing and acting.

She is the author of the Neve & Egan Cases mystery series, which features an unlikely duo of private detectives in London: Ashford Egan, a blind History professor, and Alexandra Neve, one of his students.

Currently, she is hard at work on her Urban Fantasy series Vale Investigation which chronicles the exploits of Death's only envoy on Earth, PI Bellamy Vale, in the fictitious town of Cold City, USA.

The first novel in the series, *Hostile Takeover*, won the 2019 Independent Press Award in the Urban Fantasy category.

KEEP IN TOUCH

You can sign up for Cristelle Comby's newsletter, with giveaways and the latest releases. This will also allow you to download two exclusives stories you cannot get anywhere else: *Redemption Road* (VALE INVESTIGATION prequel novella) and *Personal Favour* (NEVE & EGAN CASES prequel novella).

www.cristelle-comby.com/freebooks